Who was vandalizing the house she was building . . . and why?

After she started the car, she ran back to the house to check the doors. Once again the phone rang. This time she got it on the third ring.

"Miss Hartwell?"

"Yes."

"Hugh Perry, Mountain View Police Department. Are you building a new home on Paradise Heights?"

Ice gathered around her heart. "Yes, I am."

"Why don't you run over to the house? We'd like to talk to you."

"I'm on my way." Candy dumped the phone and ran out the door, locking it behind her.

Jumping into the car, she said nothing until her car flowed with the traffic. . . .

Chance's lips formed a hard line and the cords in his neck stood out. "What's wrong now?"

She made a left turn, her lips trembling. . . .

Silence filled the car until they reached the new subdivision and pulled up to the house. Two police cars sat at the curb and four officers walked around the house. WOMAN GO HOME! had been spray-painted in huge red letters over the entire front side of her unpainted house.

VERALEE WIGGINS is the author of more than ten novels, including *A Rose for Bethany* and *April Showers*. Ms. Wiggins makes her home in Washington State.

Books by VeraLee Wiggins

HEARTSONG PRESENTS

HP17—Llama Lady

Sweet Shelter

VeraLee Wiggins

Heartsong Presents

For you, Judy. How could I live without you?
Thank you! I love you! And God bless you
forever and ever.

ISBN 1-55748-401-5

SWEET SHELTER

one

Candace Hartwell built twelve houses in less than five years. Not bad for being only twenty-three years old. Well, not bad if she had made money on them. But she had not. In fact, she had lost money on the first ten. Lots of money. More money than she cared to admit—or even think about.

But finally she had made a profit! Not nearly enough to make up for all the thousands she had lost on the others, but at least now she had hopes of keeping herself and her seventeen-year-old sister, Judy, from starving to death and possibly even saving the family home. Her very latest house, number twelve, sold even before it was finished. She could not collect the money until the house was completed, but the buyers had put money down on it. Yesterday, she had put the final touches on the house and the sale was due to close any day. Then, she would get the check. Things definitely looked better.

She had spent some of her first-ever profit money, from the sale of house number eleven, catching up on their most pressing bills. Then, she had bought the building lot of her dreams in a fancy new subdivision called Paradise Heights, in the hills overlooking Mountain View, Washington, the small town she called home. A house in that subdivision would sell for a bundle.

When she got the check for her newly finished house, she would put some money down on the other four lots that the realtor had assured would be waiting for her when she got the money. Five fancy homes in Paradise Heights could turn her life around.

5

Candy hummed "Thank You, Lord," while turning her small faded blue Volkswagen into the new jobsite. Bliss Drive in Paradise Heights. Who wouldn't want an address like this?

Her foreman, Slade Kirkwood, and his helper, Buck Trumble, stood talking. Climbing from her car, she heard Kirkwood complaining. "I've been havin' a bad feelin' about that Mexican she hired. Now he's late—his first day of work."

"He'll be here," Candy said, approaching the two. "He's—" a small beat-up motorcycle screamed onto the lot, nearly turning over as it skidded to a halt, "here now," she finished.

Sancho Gomez dropped the kickstand, hopped off his cycle, and ran to Candy. "Sorry I'm late, Meez Hartwell. I turn east eenstead of south."

"It's all right, Sancho. Meet our foreman, Slade Kirkwood."

Sancho, whose black head lacked several inches of reaching Slade's shoulders, extended his small brown hand. "Good morning, Meester Kirkwood."

"Hope you know what yer doin'," Slade growled, ignoring the outstretched hand. "Got yer own tools?"

"Yes sir, I do." Sancho pointed to an oversized carrier on the back of his tiny cycle. "Everything I need, she's right in there."

Candy indicated the other man. "And Buck Trumble."

Buck extended his hand and the men shook hands heartily.

"Okay, Sancho, why don't you help Slade and Buck finish marking out the house? Then, we'll build the footing forms."

As the men continued the meticulous process, Candy walked around the building site. This would be a four-level house, by far the most complicated she had ever built. And the most exciting thing about it was that she knew exactly how to build it. Finally!

Her building career began five years ago when her parents died in a fiery car crash—one week after she had finished high school. Heartbroken and vulnerable, she had taken over her father's business, even though all she knew about building she'd picked up working for him during vacations. She was determined to do what she thought her father would have wanted and dropping her fully completed plans for college fit right into her "sacrifice Candy" mode.

She had poured over armloads of library books and talked to every builder she could corner. Until only recently, she had been having a difficult time passing the building inspections. Fortunately, the building inspector had been sympathetic and helpful.

Jerking back to the present, she looked at her beautifully treed lot, imagining the regal hip-roofed structure already finished. Looking beyond her lot to the four she would buy next, she envisioned four more luxurious homes, all as beautiful as the one she was beginning now. She could almost see a fancy redwood sign, HOMES BY HARTWELL.

"All squared up, Candy," Slade called, crudely breaking into her dream. "Got electricity yet?"

She scurried to string up the long electric cables.

"Hook up the saws, Buck," Slade said. "Gomez, start placing them two-by-sixes around."

"Take it easy, Sancho," Candy called laughing, as the little man took off running toward the large boards stacked under a sycamore tree. "We want you to be able to work all day."

Sancho returned with an armload of the heavy lumber. "I work hard."

"Come on, Gomez," Slade growled. "We need those

boards now."

Candy walked to her car then called Slade, who strolled over and leaned on the hood. "I need to go check on some things," she said. "You be nice to Sancho. Can't you see he's killing himself off to please you?"

"Yeah. And soon's I turn my back he'll take a siesta—or walk off with anything that ain't nailed down."

Candy scowled at Slade and climbed into her blue car, eager to visit Reva, the realtor selling her last house.

"Everything's fine," Reva said, "but it takes time to check credit, secure a bank loan, write up all the papers, and on and on. Why don't you get busy and forget this one?"

Candy sighed. "Sorry, I just wanted to be sure. I need the money bad." She didn't explain that she desperately needed to buy groceries, catch up on the payments for their home—and tie up those building lots.

The girls had received a generous settlement from their folks' death but it had all disappeared in the houses Candy had built. Sometimes, she wondered if she had done the right thing. Well, the money was gone.

She was proud of the fact that she had never doubted that God would help her learn to build. She had just kept praying, her faith never wavering, not even when one house failed its eleventh inspection. Yes, she had an abundance of faith. That was one thing of which she could surely be proud.

She drove home wondering what Judy would be doing tonight. Her wild little sister, who had finished her junior year of high school a week ago, hardly ever entertained a serious thought. Her mind ran to her looks, fun, and boys, and not necessarily in that order.

But when Candy stepped into the cool, comfortable house

no one answered her call. Hurrying to her bedroom, she showered, put on worn yellow shorts and tube top, then sank into a recliner to read the paper. Before she could finish the headlines, the doorbell interrupted her reading.

Slade Kirkwood, her foreman, stood on the porch, his steel gray hair standing on end. Must have jerked off his hat in a hurry. Tall, broad-shouldered, and lean, he reminded Candy of a much younger man but his weathered face revealed all of his fifty-odd years.

Inviting the man in, she prepared a quick meal. She felt his restlessness while she asked the blessing, but at least he bowed his head.

"Looks like we started a good one," he said a few minutes later, swallowing a mouthful of macaroni and cheese.

Candy nodded happily. "It's going to be the best I've built." She nodded again, thinking about the fantastic four-level house. "By far the best."

Slade's gray eyes narrowed and his grizzled face tightened before he relaxed and smiled. "Decided to let me build this'n my way? I can beat your time by a month."

"Slade, my friend, where were you when I couldn't pass inspections for anything and the money we got from the folks' accident dwindled and disappeared?" She poured more dressing over her salad. "I'd have loved to have had you there to teach me."

"Well, you've built four since I started and you ain't listened to nothin' I said." He reached for another serving of macaroni and cheese.

Her brown eyes softened and she touched the back of his hand. "I'm sorry. There's no doubt you know much more than I do about building. The problem is that you didn't show up until I had learned what's correct in residential building. You have this teeny little tendency to take shortcuts, and I intend to make Mountain View Construction the best outfit in the state."

"You'd do it sooner if you'd listen to me." He shook his coffee cup and drained it.

"Well, with your help we made money on the last two. The one I've collected for saved me from certain bankruptcy and paid for the new lot." She paused a moment to swallow a bite of salad. "I'm expecting the last one to close soon with a nice profit. They're still trying to foreclose on this place but, Lord willing, I'll save it, too." She smiled and offered him more coffee but he waved it away.

"Yer doin' better all right. I'm only sayin' you ain't usin' the help you're payin' for. And you're tryin' too many new-fangled ways."

Candy laughed happily. "Maybe that's why it's starting to fly. I've worked long and hard learning this business, Slade. Wasted a lot of money, too."

She shook her head thinking about how much money she had wasted. That money would have put both girls through college—and then some! Would she always wonder if she had done the right thing? Had she been unfair to Judy? She couldn't remember when either girl had had new clothes.

Slade took a long drink of milk then sighed. "You'd be a lot better off if you'd listen to me once in a while. And I'm tellin' you right now, I'm worried about that Mexican you hired." He spread a thick layer of margarine on the wheatberry bread she had retrieved from the freezer and warmed. "I got a gut feelin' he's gonna be trouble."

Candy put down her fork, wiped her mouth with a paper napkin, and smiled. "I already hired the man, so let's give him a chance. He did all right today. And don't worry about Luke.

His job's waiting for him when he gets well—even though I suspect his problems are from a bottle."

Slade nodded, looking partially relieved. He automatically reached into his shirt pocket for cigarettes she knew he wouldn't bring out in her house. His hand reappeared empty. Scraping his chair across the floor, he stood to his more than six-foot height. "Better be headin' on home. Thanks for the grub. Don't get many meals since Myrna took off."

Putting the dishes into the dishwasher, Candy heard him muttering all the way down the sidewalk. Something about not being appreciated.

The next morning she eagerly drove to the new construction site. "Looks good," she said, noticing that the footing concrete had been poured. "You're really trucking on those foundation forms."

Candy looked over the tree-covered lots, picking up on her earlier dream. She saw children playing in perfectly landscaped yards and two mothers talking over a redwood fence. "Can you believe our beautiful homes were all built by a woman?" one asked.

As Candy strained to hear the other woman's reply, a great roar drowned out her words. Locating the source of the deafening racket, she discovered a monstrous bulldozer on the next lot. For a moment, Candy felt angry at having her dream interrupted, then she came fully alive. What was that thing doing on her lot?

two

She hadn't ordered another excavation. How could she? She had barely started the house behind her. Then she remembered—that lot wasn't even hers yet. Even so, when the gargantuan machine headed for the most beautiful tree on the place, she sprang into action. Tearing past her men, she flew around her foundation and dashed up to the mammoth tractor.

"Stop!" she shrieked, waving her arms wildly. "Don't touch that tree!"

The driver looked at her, shoved the big machine into neutral, and climbed down beside her. He spat on the ground and leaned to her ear. "Something wrong?" he yelled.

"Yes. For starters you can get that thing out of here."

His eyes opened in surprise. "How come?"

Candy stood speechless. Although that lot would be hers soon she had no authority over it right now. She looked at the driver, then the bulldozer. "What are you doing, anyway?"

"Excavating for a house. What's the problem? If it's the tree, I'm taking out only that one."

Excavating for a house! How could anyone excavate for a house on a lot that wasn't even sold? Lois Paddock, the realtor, had promised those four lots to her. "I think you've made a mistake," she said. "It would be terrible to excavate the wrong place, wouldn't it?"

He pulled a crumpled sheet of paper from his pocket and read, "114 Bliss Drive, Paradise Heights?"

That would be right. Her place was 104. But someone must have gotten the address wrong. "Who hired you to do this?"

"Let's see." He pulled out the paper again. "Jeremy Chancellor." He peered at Candy over the paper. "Sound right?"

She shook her head. "I never heard of him but I guess I can't stop you."

The driver shook his head and climbed back onto his big rig.

Candy jumped into her ancient car and tore down the street. Ten minutes later, she stormed into the real estate office that had the listing on the lots.

"Lois Paddock, please," she said, barely able to stand still.

The woman at the desk glanced at a chart pinned to the wall. "She's gone," she garbled through a wad of gum. "You may be able to reach her at home."

Candy slammed into her car and drove home, praying it was a big mistake. Jerking the telephone book open, she found Paddock and dialed. A babysitter said Mrs. Paddock had made a big sale and was out celebrating with her husband. A big sale? A bare lot wouldn't be that big a deal even if it happened to be located in the most prestigious area of Mountain View.

"A penny for your thoughts, Can." Judy had come in silently and dropped to the couch beside Candy. She looked pretty in her peppermint-colored sundress and white sandals, even though both the dress and shoes showed too much wear.

"My thoughts aren't worth half a penny. What have you been doing today?"

Judy pulled back her slim shoulders. "I've been looking for a job so I can have some new clothes this fall." A shadow passed over her bright young face and the dusky blue eyes darkened. "The only thing is no one wants me to work for them."

"What kind of job are you looking for?"

Judy shrugged. "Anything a high school kid can do. I

checked a lot of fast-food places. A few stores. A couple of laundries. I'm tired of wearing the same worn-out clothes forever, Can."

Candy's heart cried a few tears knowing her sister's complaint was legitimate. But then she brightened. "A job's a great idea," she said, "but things are starting to get better with the business."

Judy nodded as though she had heard that before. Then she got up and stood before Candy.

> "I want clothes, I gotta work.
> Clothes never grew on trees.
> If I don't keepa lookin' till I find a job
> I'll just have to wear these.
> These things were fine three years ago
> But now they're all threadbare.
> Some are holey, some ripped out.
> None is fit to wear."

She bowed to Candy and reached for her hand, heading for the kitchen, "Come on, let's find something to eat. I'm starved."

Candy laughed out loud. Judy had been rhyming words long before she started to school, long long before the folks died. "How do you come up with that stuff?" she asked.

Judy shrugged. "It just comes to me."

After dinner, Candy tried a few times to call Lois Paddock. When she still wasn't home at eleven o'clock, Candy gave up trying to reach her. Omitting reading her usual Bible chapter, she said her prayers and crawled into bed. She had ordered the foundation inspection for six o'clock in the morning and the concrete pour for seven and that meant she had to get there even earlier.

Candy turned into her lot at five-fifteen in the morning and found Sancho already there. He waved a hand, but continued working over the foundation forms.

"Hi, Sancho. What are you doing?"

"Getting forms finished, Meez Hartwell. Didn't you order inspection?"

"I sure did. Also concrete. How come you didn't finish last night?"

"Meester Kirkwood had engagement. Say we finish this morning."

Candy picked up her hammer and together they moved slowly down the last wall. Slade and Buck arrived and climbed into the basement to put the finishing touches on the lower forms.

As Candy worked, she heard footsteps approach then stop beside her. At first glance she thought it was Slade, but her gaze traveled up, up, and up, until she looked into the bluest eyes she had ever seen. Blond hair curled over his forehead, hanging almost into those brilliant eyes. He wore jeans and a light blue tank top, covered with an unbuttoned red-and-blue flowered shirt. Tanned muscles rippled as he moved.

He squatted beside her. "I don't believe it," he said, shaking his head.

"What don't you believe?"

"That guy down there said you're the owner of this outfit."

Candy could hardly pull her eyes away but she knew she wouldn't be ready for the foundation inspection—not to mention the concrete pour, not to mention you don't sit and stare at people—if they didn't get these forms together now. She gave him a last glance. "Yep." She kept pounding nails into two-by-sixes.

"Hey," he said, "looks like you're in a bind. Why don't you give me that hammer?"

Candy jerked her head toward the toolshed. "They're over there."

In a moment his large tanned hands were making the work progress much faster. Soon, the last piece of rebar huddled in the forms and the last nail was set.

Candy dropped her hammer and extended her hand to the tall man. "Thanks a lot. I owe you one. I'm Candy Hartwell."

The stranger looked into Candy's eyes and accepted her extended hand. "Hi, Candy Hartwell. I'm your neighbor, Jeremy Chancellor. People call me Chance."

As they shook hands, the name sank in. Jeremy Chancellor! The guy who had allowed the desecration next door!

Jerking her hand back, she wiped it on her jeans. "What do you want?" She turned halfway around to look at the next lot. Yes, it had been excavated all right. "And what do you think you're doing over there?"

When Chance smiled, it felt as if the sun had come from behind a cloud. But he had taken her lot! "I'm building a house," he said. "I take it that's what you're doing here."

Candy didn't reply.

He cocked his head and looked at her. "I don't understand the problem. I thought building a house was a respectable thing to do." His blue eyes sparkled. "If you're a man."

"Not if you steal someone else's lot to build on. Even if you're a man." Candy felt tears welling up. Closing her eyes, she swallowed hard.

"I see. But I bought my lot just as you did. In fact, I bought all four that are ready. They're paid for and recorded at the court house. It's pretty hard to steal real estate, Candy."

All four? No wonder Paddock celebrated! So much for

depending on anyone to keep their word. She swallowed again, loudly. This guy had just destroyed her dream of building a neighborhood of fine homes. His four houses would eclipse her one, and no telling how his would look. Jumping to her feet, she squared her shoulders and gave him a withering look. "Did you want something, Mr. Chancellor?"

He hooked his thumbs in his front pockets and rocked back on his sneakers, probably size twenty-two. "Well, yes, I was wondering if I could borrow some electricity. Mine isn't turned on."

She should say no. But she really couldn't, even though he had taken her lots. All four of them! She jerked her head toward the pole. "Help yourself."

As he walked away, the building inspector arrived in his city-owned pick-up truck. "Well, Candy, looks like you've started a dandy this time," Henry Hadleigh said, smiling fondly at her.

"Oh, I don't know, Henry," a rich baritone voice said with a chuckle. "You'd better check her out. You know, since she's only a woman." Chance shook hands with the inspector and fell into step beside him.

Where did that big ape come from? But as Candy walked behind him she noticed he didn't look much like an ape. He looked more like a—hey, she could see daylight between his knees as he walked. Mr. Perfect was bowlegged! But what was he doing here?

The building inspector dropped back beside Candy. "It looks great, Candy. Now—"

"But, Henry," Chance interrupted, slowing so they had to walk beside him, "what about that unfinished section in the basement?"

Hadleigh sighed. "I know the lady, Chancellor. In fact, I taught her how to build."

"Well, don't you think the house is a little small for the neighborhood?"

Hadleigh looked surprised. "No, I don't and it isn't. It's well over the covenant specifications. And don't worry, she's an extremely competent builder."

Candy couldn't have been more pleased. "Thanks, Henry," she said, smiling. Then to Chance, "Now, why don't you go over and make sure your own forms are getting built right?"

The tall man strode away.

The building inspector finished and climbed into his pickup.

"See you when I get it framed," she called, then ran to the basement to help.

About midafternoon, when the concrete had been poured and her men had everything under control, she wandered off to study the blueprints—and her competitor. She opened her car door and leaned on the seat studying the blueprints. Fifteen minutes later she opened the spec book.

"You really head this operation?" a deep voice asked.

Candy looked up into *those* eyes. "What's so strange about me heading this thing?" she snapped.

Chance held his hand out in front of him as though to shield himself. "Take it easy. I only meant that you're such a tiny little thing. You look fragile enough to break in a breeze and this. . . ."

"I'm not interested in your flattery," Candy said, interrupting. "Is that how you managed to weasel those lots away?"

"Ah, now I'm beginning to catch on." Chance pulled a large red kerchief from his pocket and mopped his face. "You wanted the lots for yourself. Did you have money on them?"

She wanted to scream that she certainly did. "No," she

whimpered.

"Well, no one told me someone else was interested in them."

Candy tried to read her spec book.

He lifted the book from her hands, leaned over, and looked into her eyes. "Mmm. Soft chocolate candy. Are you like your eyes? Or are you peppermint candy, sweet but spicy?"

"What?"

"Your eyes. They're the softest, sweetest eyes I've ever seen."

"Why don't you go build your house?"

Chance laughed. "What's your house like? I hope it won't destroy the neighborhood." He looked as serious as a tumble down a sixty-foot embankment. But his laughing eyes gave him away.

"Don't worry about my house," she said. "It's top drawer. That's what I've been yelling about. I wanted to build a community of fantastic homes. So what about your wonderful house?"

He leaned past her into the car, retrieved the blueprints she'd been studying and looked them over. "Not too bad," he said, "but a little small."

"Two thousand, nine hundred ninety square feet is too small? How big is yours?"

He raised an eyebrow. "Three thousand three hundred square feet. I suppose I couldn't expect more from an inexperienced builder—and a woman."

Candy knew perfectly well he was teasing but she wasn't in the mood. "Go home, big man," she said. "Go home and build your wonderful house. All four wonderful houses. Just get out of my sight before I throw up."

Chance clicked his sneakers together and saluted. "Right.

All four. See you later, Peppermint Candy."

He had dumped his red-and-blue shirt somewhere and, as he walked away, Candy watched the muscles in his back and arms ripple in the blue tank top. He needs a haircut, she thought, as the breeze rustled his sunshine-colored hair. But why was she standing here watching him? She had better things to do.

Much later, Candy walked around her foundation. The basement looked like a swimming pool and the ground level resembled a roller-skating rink.

"Who tells you how?" Chance asked, falling into step with her.

"Who tells me how what? And what are you doing back on my property?" Candy, feeling as though she had been running hard, stopped and leaned against a tree.

Chance propped a big foot on a pile of two-by-six ends. "Who tells you how to build a house?" he asked.

"Nobody tells me how. Ask those guys over there if I know how to build a house."

"Why? Why did you choose to be a builder? Why not a secretary?" He looked her up and down. "Or an actress?" He picked a twig off the tree and broke it into inch-long pieces.

"What are you saying? That a woman isn't smart enough to be a builder?"

As he met her gaze, his eyes opened wide. "No, that's not what I meant to say. I'd better get to work before I put my other foot in my mouth. Come over and see me sometime." He returned to his lot where the foundation forms looked nearly finished.

Candy checked her watch—four o'clock. Not much left to do this afternoon.

She told her men goodbye and trudged toward her car, only to be intercepted once more by Jeremy Chancellor.

"You really should reconsider building that little cracker box," he said, leaning against the door of her car.

"What am I supposed to do," she asked, ignoring his outrageously twinkling eyes, "rip out the foundation and start over? All for about three hundred square feet?"

"Three hundred square feet is a huge room." Only the tiny twitch at the left corner of his mouth gave away his light mood. "It could make the difference between a house selling or sitting."

"I'll put my house up against yours any day of the week," she said. "Now, if you'll move your big carcass I'd like to go home."

A car driving in interrupted the conversation. Judy. Why would she be here?

Judy jumped out of her car and slammed the door shut. As she trotted over to Candy, her short blond curls bounced around her face.

"Hi, Candy. I have a message from Reva." Judy stopped and looked from Candy to Chance and back. "Sorry, I didn't realize you had company."

"It's okay, Judy. What did Reva say?"

"She said to tell you the house closing will be delayed about a week, but not to worry." Judy looked up at Chance. "Hi, handsome," she sang out. "I'm Judy Hartwell."

Chance looked at Candy questioningly, but receiving no response, returned his attention to Judy. "Hello, Judy Hartwell," he said. "I'm Jeremy Chancellor. Let's see now. Hartwell." He glanced at Candy and smiled broadly, his eyes twinkling mischievously. "Mother and daughter?"

Judy laughed; Candy didn't. "Close," Judy said. "She's

been my mother since our parents died. We're sisters."

An amazed look spread over Chance's face. "I'll bet this was your father's business."

Candy smiled thinly. "You win. Pick up the marbles."

"What were you talking about, anyway?" Judy asked.

"I was making a jerk of myself," Chance said.

"Come on, what were you doing?"

"Nothing," Candy said, "just talking about our houses. Chance is building on the next lot, where those men are."

Judy looked. "Oh. That's the lot you were climbing the walls about last night."

Chance said nothing but listened attentively.

"He's the one who bought the lot, yes," Candy said. "In fact, he bought all four lots."

"Wow!" Judy looked from one to the other. "You were fighting." She twinkled up at Chance. "Well, I'm not mad at you. Why don't you come over for dinner tonight?"

"Judy!" As Candy's face reddened, she became painfully aware of her dirty jeans, faded rumpled shirt, sweaty body, and the dark tangled mess she called hair. But why should she care about how she looked? She had just put in a hard day and this big jerk hadn't made it any easier.

For only a moment, he looked embarrassed. Then his discomfort changed to playfulness. "Well, thanks," he said, grinning at Judy. "I'm starved."

Enough was enough. "You can eat anywhere you want, Jeremy Chancellor, except at my place." Then, "Go home, Judy. I'll see you there in twenty minutes."

Judy smiled broadly, ran to her car, turned, and threw kisses with both hands. Candy held her breath for fear Judy would start spouting poetry—about the handsome man no doubt. But she merely hopped into her car and eased to the street.

Chance whistled. "Quite a girl."

"Yes," Candy agreed, "quite." Inside, she seethed. Why did Judy have to act like that? And how could she expect to control someone who weighed thirty pounds more than she and stood six inches taller?

Candy glanced up to find Chance gazing tenderly at her. As their eyes met, he put his hand on her shoulder. "Don't worry about Judy. Before you know it, she'll be all grown up."

Candy moved away, causing his hand to drop to his side. Now why did she do that? He was only being kind. And it wasn't his fault he had bought her lots. Usually she prided herself on her fairness, but this time she was way out of line.

Chance raised his eyebrows and Candy burst out laughing. "I'm mad at you for buying my lots," she said, still giggling. "It wasn't your fault, but I can't help it. And Judy didn't help my frame of mind much, either."

"You aren't mad," he answered kindly. "You're disappointed. I'm sorry I messed up your plans, but I'm glad I'm building up here—and met you." He trudged slowly to his property.

Just then, a small car drove up. A large dark-haired man approached and Candy met him halfway.

"Hello, Miss Hartwell?" He smiled, exposing a broken tooth, and extended his hand to her. "I'm Pete Meyer. Does the name ring a bell?"

Candy shook her head and his hand. "Sorry. Should it?" She moved over to her new foundation and sat down on it.

Pete Meyer lowered himself to sit beside her. "Well, that may be for the best. What I'd like is a job. You see, your dad fired me just before . . . you know. The thing is, someone lied about me. The inspector found half the nails on one end of the siding missing. Someone said I had done it but I hadn't even worked on that part of the building. Dave fired me on the spot."

"What an awful thing to happen!" Candy exclaimed. "But we have a full crew—Pete, was it?"

"Yeah." He hunched over, looking angry. "But I can't get another job in this town. Somehow everyone knows about that rotten incident and believes I'm undependable."

Candy thought a moment. She absolutely couldn't dole out any charity right now. "I'm sorry, Pete, but I can't hire anyone else. I'm just starting to make money, and I can't take the chance. We already have one more man than Dad ever hired."

The big man lurched to his feet, face red and eyes flashing. "Why should you help someone your dad ruined?" he said much louder than necessary. "It's not your responsibility, is it? Well, listen to this and listen good." As he talked, his voice kept growing louder and louder. "You're going to wish you'd helped someone just this one time, you rich, stuck-up broad. I promise you that."

three

Pete Meyer stormed to his car, slammed the door, and roared away.

Candy didn't blame him for being unhappy, but if she didn't watch it, *she'd* be out begging for a job.

When she arrived home, she paused to appreciate the fantastic feeling of finishing a good day's work.

"Hi. You look beat," Judy sang out while coming from the kitchen. "I have supper started. Can," she rolled her eyes, "have you ever seen such a hunk?"

Brother, Candy didn't need this. "Who do you mean?" she asked.

Judy whirled around. "You know who I mean."

"Leave him alone, Judy. He's way too old for you." Candy edged toward the bathroom. "How do you think God felt about your performance today?" she had to add.

Judy glared into Candy's eyes. "Do you have any idea how sick I get of that question?" she snapped. "You've been doing that to me as long as I can remember. I'm not a baby, Can, and what's more I think God understands me a lot better than you do. Besides all that, I'm sure He loves me. Sometimes I wonder about you." She stormed back to the kitchen so Candy ran for the shower.

A half hour later she emerged from her bedroom, feeling fresh and a lot more human, in blue shorts, blouse, and sandals.

"I thought you'd never get out of there," Judy said warmly as if they hadn't just had words. "I have a surprise. Don't move." A moment later, she returned with a large plate of taco salad. Handing it to Candy, she went after a duplicate serving for herself.

Candy enjoyed several crunchy bites. "This is nice," she said. "Kind of calming. I had a bad day."

Judy nodded. "If I worked next door to Jeremy Chancellor I'd come home pooped too."

Candy scooped up a bite of tomato. "Well, in the first place I worked like crazy getting the forms ready for inspection. Then, of course, we had the pour to take care of and all that flatwork was killing. Lastly, Jeremy Chancellor has been a pain all day. I'd be happy never to see him again."

Judy picked up a piece of paper from the table and gave Candy a strange look. "Listen, Can. I wrote something for you," she said.

"So you had a bad day.
Maybe someone hurt your feelings,
Called you a glutton and a drunkard?
Not that? But you had a bad day.
Did someone follow you around trying to trick you
Into saying something that would land you in jail?
No? I guess no one would do that, would they?
But you still had a bad day.
Did some of your children ask you to love them
More than you love their siblings?
Oh. I suppose no one would do that.
I know. You still had a bad day.
Maybe you overworked. Did someone force you
To carry a heavy cross through town and up a hill?
Finally, you grew so tired you collapsed.
Not that? Well, I understand something like that has
    happened.
I'm sorry about your bad day. Did someone hurt you?

Flog you with a leaded whip? Shove a crown of large
thorns onto your head?
Pound enormous nails into your hands and feet?
Now that's a bad day.
That wasn't it, either?
Come, tell me about your bad day.
You don't remember what caused your bad day?
You don't remember having a bad day?
God Bless, and may all your tomorrows be better."

Candy could hardly believe that had come from Judy—her
little sister who made every excuse to skip church. Who never
had a serious thought in her life. Well, it certainly demonstrated
how bad *her* bad day wasn't. She felt about as tall as a
nightcrawler that had just stumbled over a speck of dust.

"Okay," she said when she caught her breath, "so I didn't
have a bad day. Where'd you get that, anyway?"

Judy shook her head. "I think I was getting even with you for
asking what God would think of me. I'm sorry, Can. Want an
ice cream cone?" She got up with her empty plate. "I saw some
tin roof sundae in the freezer."

"Okay, thanks." As Candy waited for the ice cream, she
realized that Judy not only had a serious thought, but knew
something of what Jesus had gone through. And besides all that,
Judy could be right about something else. Candy wasn't sure
she minded Chance's visits as much as she had indicated.

A few minutes later, Judy returned with tall chocolate cones
and handed one to Candy before dropping into the rocker. "I'm
glad you don't like Chance," she said, licking all the way
around her cone, " 'cause I'm going after him."

Candy choked on a bite of melted ice cream. Then, "You're
not going after him, Judy! You're just a kid."

Judy took another lick. "You'd be happy never to see him again, right?"

"Right."

"And you don't like him even a little, right?"

"Right."

Judy jumped in front of Candy. "Have you ever heard of the dog in the manger, Can? The dog didn't like hay, but he jumped into the manger and wouldn't let the cow have it either. Does that remind you of anyone, Can?" Candy had no answer so Judy sat back down.

That night, Candy thanked the Lord for helping her learn to build houses and also for helping a little religion sink into Judy's head. Then, she asked Him to forgive her for being unkind to Chance. Immediately, she realized she must apologize to the man.

The next morning she and her crew pulled the forms from the drying foundation. "You may as well go on home," Candy said, when the last board lay on the ground. "Take care of all your personal business. I intend to keep you busy for the next couple of months. We'll start Monday."

"I'm gone," Buck said.

"Thanks, Candy." Slade followed Buck away.

"I help you, Meez Hartwell," Sancho said. "These boards too heavy for you. You don't pay me. I just help."

"Of course, I'll pay you," Candy said. "And, thanks."

"Where do you live while working in the States, Sancho?" Candy asked as they carried the heavy boards.

"Anywheres, Meez Hartwell. Right now, I live in house trailer on old highway." He raised his black eyebrows. "The rent, she's free and if anybody don't like me there I can move. All I have is my clothings."

Candy remembered seeing the abandoned trailer, with a large section of wall missing, sitting down from the highway, partially hidden by brush.

By noon, they had all the forms neatly stacked. Sancho climbed onto his ancient cycle and chugged away.

Candy walked around the foundation, double-checking to be sure she had ordered the right amount of each kind of lumber.

"Relax, Peppermint Candy. It's not going anywhere."

Jerking to a stop, she looked up into those deep blue eyes. "I was double-checking for the material that's coming this afternoon," she explained. "I'm eager to get this house finished and sold, so I can't afford to lose any time waiting on reorders."

He stood with his feet apart and thumbs tucked into jeans pockets—the picture of innocence. "Well, why didn't you say so? Get your materials' list and blueprints. I'll help you."

"I don't need any help. You must be about ready for inspection now."

"Yeah, we are," he said. "Why don't you come over and see?"

"I'm busy."

Snatching her hand, he walked her toward his place. "I come over all the time and you never return my visits. You're having a look at my house, now."

Eager to see his blueprints, Candy meekly followed her imprisoned hand. Three shirtless men looked up, grinned, and returned to pounding big nails into long boards.

Chance picked up a set of blueprints, shook the dust off, and carried it to the shade of a sycamore tree. Squatting, he laid the papers on the ground. Using a small stick, he pointed to the picture on the front. "The house is pretty mod—has gable ends all over the place."

Candy took a quick look through the plans and discovered

it amazingly like the one she had started.

"Don't you wish you were building a nice house like this?" he asked.

She burst out laughing. "You're crazy. They'll look enough alike to have been built by the same builder. By the way, I'm sorry I was mean to you yesterday."

"Apology accepted. Forgiven and forgotten." They talked a few more minutes before Candy had to leave.

The weekend passed quietly and Candy especially enjoyed the sermon at church on Sunday. The minister's message was this: Work hard to keep your faith strong so that when trials do come along, you can stand. Well, that was one thing she didn't have to worry about. She might not have much money and she might need some more knowledge about building houses but faith was the one thing she had in great supply.

Too bad Judy hadn't come to church with her. Lately, it was getting harder and harder to get Judy out to church. In fact, as she thought about it, it was getting harder to get Judy to do anything she didn't want to.

Monday morning, Judy ran into Candy's bedroom. "Look what I found stuck in the door." She held a piece of wrinkled paper between her thumb and index finger as though it were contaminated.

Candy took the paper, smoothed it out, and read the typed message:

HARTWELL—GO HOME. NO ROOM FOR YOU IN A MAN'S WORLD. HOT SHOT WOMAN CANT BILD GOOD ENUFH FOR PARDISE HITES.

Candy turned shocked eyes to Judy. "Did you see who put

it there?"

Judy shook her head and spoke in a hushed voice. "It fell down when I opened the door."

Candy couldn't tear her eyes from the ugly message. She had had no idea anyone felt that way about her. Pete Meyer! The man who had threatened her when she couldn't give him a job. Was he really that upset? Who else could it have been? Who else was building up there? Jeremy Chancellor!

"Judy, do you think it's Chance?"

"No!" Judy said. "Don't even say it. But it's someone," she added in a frightened whisper.

Candy tossed the ugly little paper onto her night stand. "Don't mention this to anyone," she said. "We'll think about it today, and talk again tonight." When Candy left for work, she could tell she was leaving an upset little sister.

Candy arrived on the job at six-forty-five, the last one to arrive. Even Luke Loomis was there looking healthy. "Hi, guys," Candy said. "Welcome back, Luke. Okay, let's get this one finished in record time. By tomorrow night I'd like to have all the basement walls up and the living area sub-flooring on."

Glancing over to Chance's place, Candy noticed the building inspector. He and Chance shook hands and Henry walked toward her house.

"Hello there, Candy," he called. "I see you're starting to put wood on. I have faith that you'll build this one with no problems just as you did last time. Even though it's more complicated. I can't believe how you've learned in the last few years."

As they talked, a rustle attracted Candy's attention, then Chance appeared. "I hope you aren't talking about me," he said, looking from Henry to Candy. She detected a sparkle in his eyes and the left corner of his lip twitched.

"Oh, no," the inspector said, "we'd forgotten all about you."

Chance stuck his hands in his pockets. She looked at him carefully as he talked to Henry Hadleigh. Could he write a nasty note like the one Judy found?

"Well, if you're passing out building tips, I'll take some," Chance said.

Hadleigh flustered a bit and left. Chance burst out laughing as the inspector drove away.

"What's so funny?" Candy asked.

"Oh, Candy, you must know you're a beautiful woman. Also a feisty little thing with lots of fire—like peppermint candy. I admire you and want to be your friend. Obviously, Henry feels the same way."

"I doubt that," Candy said. "Anyway, I don't have time for men."

Chance grinned. "Sure you do." He looked down the road after Hadleigh. "Hopefully, he won't be back until one of us gets our house framed. No doubt that'll be mine."

Candy's eyes flashed. "And why would yours be framed first? I'm ahead and I plan to stay that way."

Chance looked almost drowsy, his eyes nearly closed. "You're pretty savvy—for a woman," he purred, "but I'd bet a lot of money on my know-how opposed to your beginner's luck." He turned and strode to his own house.

Maybe he did write that note. He had plenty to say about her femininity. It always seemed like a joke but maybe he had some kind of problem.

Candy barely began looking over her crew's work when Chance returned, carrying one end of a long electrical cord. "My electricity's turned on now. May I return what I borrowed?" he asked.

Candy laughed. "Idiot! Keep your electricity. You're going to need it before this is all over."

After Chance walked a few feet, Candy remembered the note. "Do you have a typewriter?" she called.

He spun around. "Sure do. Want to use it?"

"No, I guess not."

He walked away, shaking his head.

Returning to her own place, Candy found most of the joists secured. She enjoyed the physical labor involved in building and tomorrow she would be nailing subflooring. She hurried to the toolshed where she found nail guns but no nails.

A half hour later, she drove to the shed to unload enough nails and staples to do the whole house. Struggling with the heavy boxes she wished for the millionth time that she were bigger and stronger.

"Why are you doing that?"

Candy turned to find Chance holding a small gray suitcase in his right hand. He set it down, took the box from her hands, and carried it into the toolshed. "These things are heavy. Why aren't your men doing this?" After carrying all the boxes into the shed, he picked up the suitcase and placed it in her hands.

"What's this?" she asked.

He grinned lazily down at her. "It's more your size, isn't it?"

She turned the case and read: SMITH CORONA. He had brought his typewriter! Now what? She needed that like she needed the awful note. But, wait! She could compare the printing from this typewriter with the note.

"Thanks," she said. "I appreciate this more than you know. I'll bring it back tomorrow."

four

He would never have brought the typewriter if he had used it to write the note, Candy thought as she drove home. *Well, he might have, just to allay my suspicions.*

Judy met her at the door and was unusually quiet for her. "Do you know who did it, Can?" she whispered

Candy could tell this morning's note still shook up her big little sister a lot. She lifted the gray case high and grinned. "No, but I have Chance's typewriter. We'll compare the type."

After typing the message and comparing the papers under the fluorescent kitchen light, Judy looked at Candy in shock. "See, Can," she said, "even the little squiggles are alike. Look at the *G*. The *A* matches, too. Everything matches!"

Candy felt her throat tighten. "I guess we know who wrote the note," she said, trying to regulate her breathing.

Judy swallowed loudly but said nothing.

"No, we don't," Candy said. "There are probably millions of typewriters around here just like Chance's."

"Right," Judy whispered, "it doesn't mean a thing."

A few minutes later, as the shower beat on Candy's back, she thought over the events of the day. It had been a pretty good day as far as progress on the house went. Chance had acted decently. Slade hadn't persecuted Sancho much. Yes, it had been a good day.

Thinking about Judy's bad day poem, she decided it had been a great day. How could she complain when her Savior had gone through so much for her? And He had done it because He loved her and the rest of His children so much He couldn't bear to see them lost. She couldn't even understand a love like that, but she

34

could appreciate it. "Thank You, God," she whispered.

The next morning, Candy put the typewriter into Chance's van and thanked him for the loan.

"You're welcome," he said. "Use it anytime."

Candy took a deep breath. "Have you used it lately?"

He looked surprised at the question. "Yeah, whenever I need something I can't order over the phone."

"Well, I'd better get to work. I'm nailing subfloor today. Thanks again."

She walked back to her house trying to convince herself that Chance didn't and couldn't write the note. She collected her nail gun, climbed onto the floor, and nailed down the three-quarter-inch plywood the men had positioned. The gun was heavy and she worked fast, bent over with legs straight, so, after a couple of hours, her back demanded a rest. She climbed down, struggled to a shady spot under the trees, and flopped into the soft green weeds. Resting quietly, she noticed the sound of large machines in the distance, then closed her eyes for a few more minutes.

Almost as soon as she returned to shooting nails into the plywood, Chance knelt beside her. Her heart pounded in competition with the nail gun so she turned it off—the gun, not her heart—and dropped to a sitting position on the new floor.

"Oh, no you don't," Chance said, grinning like a dog with two bones. "Get up and come with me."

Candy continued sitting until he grasped her hand and jerked her unceremoniously off the four-foot edge.

Candy's breath came quickly. "What do you think you're doing?"

He still grinned. "Shut up and listen."

She shut up and listened. In a moment, she heard the big machines again. She raised an eyebrow and looked at Chance.

He turned her around and pointed in the distance. "See that."

"I see, but what is it?"

"They're developing the next five lots. I was hoping this would help you forgive me for taking these."

Candy felt sudden elation. Maybe she could build her little community after all. Chance's houses would fit right in. Maybe they could sort of do it together. Whoa! She didn't need help— from anyone.

She raised worried brown eyes to Chance's eager blue ones. "I don't have any money until my last house closes. I suppose you plan to grab those lots before I get my money."

Chance nodded soberly. "I hadn't thought about it but I'm always on the lookout for nice lots. Always." The left corner of his lip gave a single twitch. "Why don't we discuss it over dinner tonight?"

"How can we talk?" she wailed. "I don't have any money. And I don't enjoy having a rich chauvinist pig lording it over me." She ran back and started nailing flooring again.

As she worked, she thought about Chance. He probably didn't know how it was to struggle for anything. Why didn't that house hurry up and close, anyway?

"You turned him down?" Judy yelled when Candy told her about the new lots. "He asked you out for dinner and you refused? You really are losing it, Can. I'll get him to ask me out. Unless you think he wrote the note?"

"Of course he didn't," Candy said with more assurance than she felt. "But you leave him alone, anyway."

The next morning, as Candy and her crew began work, Judy drove up. "Looks good, Can. Hey, I'm going over to your neighbor's place."

"No way, Judy. You go right back home."

A brilliant smile covered Judy's tanned face as she marched toward Chance's foundation.

Candy returned to her nailing. She shouldn't have let Judy go over there. But she didn't! This was exactly what she had been dreading—Judy outright defying her command. Where would it all go from here?

Unable to concentrate on the wall she was building, she dropped her hammer and ran next door where Chance's crew was putting the first wood on his house. Judy stood on the far side of the foundation, talking to Chance. As Candy rounded the corner to join them, it looked as if he were enjoying the visit altogether too much.

Candy tried to smile. "Hi, guys," she called. "Judy, are you keeping Chance from work?"

Chance barely glanced at Candy. "No, we're fine. Just getting acquainted." Then, he returned his attention to the tall blond girl.

Candy noticed, not for the first time, how really pretty Judy was. Super large blue eyes set far apart in her square face. Her wide mouth parted in a smile, revealing white, even teeth. Her features weren't delicate by any means, but altogether she made a striking picture. Lean, tanned legs that went on forever supported her supple body.

"Uh, I hate to interrupt," Candy said, "but I want you to go call in this order for me, Judy. Right away." She held a mutilated sheet of notebook paper to Judy, who accepted it.

Chance snatched it from Judy's hand. "No need. I have a phone here. Saves lots of gas." He handed it back to Candy. "You're welcome to use it, anytime." Gesturing in the general direction of the phone, he returned his attention to Judy.

Candy plodded to the phone. Now what? She didn't need that

stuff for several more days anyway and she couldn't allow Judy to continue flaunting herself before Chance.

Retracing her steps, she found the two still talking. "Judy, I want you to go home right now. You have things to do."

Judy turned her back almost directly toward Candy as she laughed up into Chance's face.

He glanced around Judy and met Candy's eyes. "Well, I've had my break," he said. "I'd better get to work. Take care." He walked off leaving the girls together.

Judy wheeled to face Candy, her eyes hard. "Now see what you did! He was about to ask me out, too." She flounced away, climbed into her car, and disappeared in a cloud of dust.

Candy smiled to herself. At least Judy had gone home. How long she would stay there was another matter—this new Judy who didn't obey her anymore.

When Candy got back to her house, the guys had one wall up. Before the day ended, all the walls on the ground level would be standing and it would begin to look like a house.

In less than an hour, Judy pulled up to Chance's place again. She had barely had time to go home! She jumped out, looking gorgeous in bright red bib overalls and a sunshiny yellow blouse. Candy stood up to watch her sister approach Chance. She couldn't hear what they said, but Judy laughed and gestured as she talked. Chance listened, then grinned, made some strange motions, and laughed loudly. He put down his hammer and stood with Judy, laughing with her about something Candy couldn't fathom.

Candy snatched her hammer and a large nail, and proceeded to smash her thumb. Dropping the hammer she watched a bright blue color creep over the entire thumbnail. Trying to ignore the pain, she nailed the rest of the studs tightly between the long boards. Tears ran from her eyes and nose.

A little later, she looked up to see Pete Meyer, the man who had asked for a job, leaning against a tree watching her. When their eyes met, he approached. "You don't look very happy," he said, quietly.

Candy grinned. "Very astute, Pete. I just smashed my thumb." She held it up for inspection.

Peter whistled. "That's a bad one. You should let the blood out with a needle."

"Through the fingernail?"

"Yes. It relieves the pressure—and pain. Why don't you let me take your place? I work hard."

"I can't let a little pain stop me," she said. "Really, Pete, I'd like to hire you, but you can see I have enough workers."

A giant crash, followed by tinkling glass, stopped the conversation.

Candy and Pete, along with her four men, rushed to the garage area, where the long north wall lay in a heap on the concrete floor. The fall smashed the windows and pulled the studs from the sill board.

Candy looked at Slade, who looked at Sancho.

Slade's eyes turned to slits. "It's that dumb Mexican," he snarled. "Never done nothin' right yet."

Sancho's eyes widened. "But Meester Kirkwood, don't you. . . ?"

"Don't say nothin'," Slade interrupted. "Just get out of here— now!"

Candy's mouth dropped open. Since when did Slade fire her men? Sancho walked away, head bowed, and rode off on his tiny cycle.

Pete Meyer stepped to her side. "So . . . you have a place for me," he said. "I can start, now."

She shook her head. "Sorry, Pete. No can do."

He looked at her with disbelief, then understanding. "I see," he muttered. "You don't believe me, do you? Well, you and your house can just disappear with my blessings. You never know how soon that will be, either."

Watching him angrily slam his car door, Candy wondered again if he had written that awful note. She shuddered. The next thing she knew, he would burn her place down as his threat insinuated.

Late in the afternoon Judy's car pulled in again, much slower. What did the girl think? That she lived out here?

"Candy," Judy called, softly. "I have bad news."

Bad news? "What is it?" Candy asked, laying her hammer between two studs.

"It's your house over on Beaumont. The sale fell through."

"Oh, no! Did she say what happened?"

"No. Just that she wanted to talk to you as soon as possible."

"Okay, I'm on my way. Why don't you ride over with me?"

"I have someone to visit. If you aren't here, maybe I'll get somewhere."

Candy didn't like the idea of Judy messing around Chance's place but the girl was too big to spank and too strong to push into a car, so she took off, alone.

"We tried every kind of creative financing possible," Reva said, "but it finally boiled down to bad credit."

"That money was to catch up on our personal home payments and some other vital stuff."

"Another party wanted the house," the real estate agent continued, kindly. "I'll try to run that down in the morning."

Candy stood up. "I'll say a prayer for that."

When she got home, Judy met her at the door wearing a big smile and looking innocent. Candy didn't feel like smiling.

Wordlessly, she held out her thumb for Judy's inspection.

Judy took it in her hands. "Wow, how'd you ever do that?" She gently moved the injured hand back to Candy. "I hope I don't do that."

"Smashed thumbs aren't a top priority worry item for you, are they?"

Judy, eyes innocent, dropped her bomb. "I want to work for you, Can," she said eagerly. "I'm bigger and stronger than you, so I know I can handle it."

"Oh, Judy, I'm hungry. Can't we talk about this later?" Candy raised one eyebrow. "Maybe next year?"

Judy pushed Candy onto the couch. "Let's just get this settled before we eat. You worked several summers for Dad while you were in high school."

"I remember. But I didn't have my eye on some bozo nearby. If I hired you, you'd be next door flirting with the competition."

"Unfair, Can. I promise never to go over there during work time. In fact—I'll work so hard I break my back, and won't take time to eat a snack."

"I have a full crew, Judy. Four is perfect. And I make five. I turned a guy away twice in the last few days and he got really mad. Scared me, in fact."

Judy jumped up. "Okay, let's eat. I'm not going to get mad. If you can't hire me, you can't. I'll ask Chance."

Candy lost her appetite, hardly sampling the fancy cold cucumber sandwiches Judy had made. She pushed the macaroni salad around in her plate for a few minutes, then excused herself.

Barely able to sleep due to the pounding thumb and Judy's brainstorm, Candy struggled out of bed exhausted the next morning and put on a touch of lipstick, something she hadn't done before, just for work.

five

"Please," Candy said as they cleared away the breakfast dishes, "forget asking Chance for a job."

A small frown replaced Judy's smile. "I already mentioned it to him."

"So! What did he say?"

"He seemed real interested."

"I'll bet, after your performance yesterday."

"He's not like you think, Can," Judy said. "He's a nice guy."

"Sure he is," Candy snapped. "I don't want you to take the job. It isn't right for a girl to work with a bunch of rough guys."

Judy laughed. "Do you realize how dumb that sounds, coming from you?"

"I call the shots where I work. If someone gets out of line, he's gone. You'll be stuck with . . . whatever. Do you understand?"

"Sure. But don't worry, Can, Chance won't let anyone bother me. I'm hoping *he'll* harass me a little, though."

"I'm forbidding you to take the job, Judy."

Judy dropped to the floor in front of Candy's chair and took her good hand. "You can't do that, Can. You couldn't hire me. I've tried every place in Mountain View. This is my chance to earn some money."

Candy's thumb throbbed until she could barely think. "I know things are tough," she said, "but they'll get better."

"I'm not complaining. I just want some clothes."

Candy, inwardly admitting defeat, struggled to her feet, dragged herself to the bathroom, and prepared for work.

As soon as Chance climbed out of his white van, Candy stormed over to talk to him. "I don't want Judy working here. The atmosphere isn't right for a young girl."

Chance leaned on a low sycamore limb. "My crew's almost as civilized as yours."

"You're not to hire her, understand?"

He sifted a handful of dust through his long lean fingers. "Why don't you tell her she isn't to work for me?"

Her brown eyes looked beseechingly into his. "I can't handle her."

Chance took his time digesting the surprising news that Candy couldn't do everything. Then, he straightened up and wiped his hand on his jeans. "Why don't you tell me the real reason you don't want her working here?"

"It's not a good place for her. Tell me you won't hire her."

Chance grinned lazily down at Candy. "Well, I don't know. I'm a firm believer in equality for women. Say! Why don't we discuss the problem at dinner tonight? After we eat you can itemize the reasons you don't want Judy working for me. If your reasons are valid, I won't hire her."

"Oh, not this again. You believe in equality? I call what you're doing to me sexual harassment."

Why didn't she feel better after that tirade? Why did she feel she had been mean to a nice person? Her conscience hurt worse than her thumb.

After waiting a moment, he nodded. "Okay, I'll have to use my best judgment." His eyes laughed at her although his lips remained still—except the telltale twitch at the corner.

Candy's thumb kept her from putting her heart into her work. As she sat under a tree resting, Buck Trumble joined her. "The breeze feels good, doesn't it?" he asked pleasantly after sitting down in the soft grass and weeds beside her.

"Sure does," she said.

He looked at the fat blue thumb. "That looks sore. You shouldn't be here. Say, Candy, you know the wall that fell yesterday? Well, I have to tell you, Slade hurried us to the next one before that one was stable. Sancho insisted the wall wasn't secure, but Slade told him to shut up and get to work."

Candy nodded. "I see. I'll go find Sancho right now. I won't forget this, Buck."

Sancho didn't answer Candy's knock, so she left a note on the trailer door inviting him back to work.

When she returned to work she called Slade aside. "I know I'm being a baby," she said, "but I'm taking the rest of the day off."

Slade examined her hand and gave a low whistle. "You're not being a baby," he assured her. "You go home and I'll carry on here."

Candy smiled her thanks. "Oh, yes," she said, "Sancho's coming back to work. We don't want to be responsible for a bunch of hungry kids. He'll be extra careful now. Be good to him, okay?"

He patted her on the shoulder. "If Gomez is your charity of the year, I guess I can take it," he said with a small smile.

"Thanks. You're the greatest." Candy stood on tiptoe and brushed the whiskery chin with a kiss, then headed for her car.

As she pulled the car door open, she noticed Judy's car on Chance's lot. What was she doing here? Then her eyes fell on a bright yellow patch of movement. What was she doing anyway? Candy had to watch only a moment to deduce that her big little sister was working. Working for Chance.

After driving home like a maniac, Candy slammed her front door soundly. How could those two flout her instructions so flagrantly? She took three aspirins and crawled into bed.

After a long afternoon and longer night, the swelling in her thumb subsided, although the nail looked as brightly colored as ever. Waggling it painfully, she decided she could work. She put on a bit of makeup and a pair of older red dress pants with a soft pink sleeveless blouse. Maybe if she looked better she would feel better.

When she turned into her place, she noticed two picnic tables, each about eight-feet long, sitting in the shade under her trees. She idly wondered who put them there—and why.

As she closed her car door, Chance met her. "Are the tables all right?"

Candy glanced at them once more. "All right for what?"

"For lunch. I thought if we all ate our lunches together you'd feel more comfortable about Judy. That'll be her only free time, you know. Oh, by the way, she's catching on much faster than I dared hope."

"Is that right? Well, you can't imagine how relieved I am about that." Turning her back on Jeremy Chancellor, she hurried away to start her day's work.

He didn't even mention her thumb. Probably forgot all about it.

"Hey, Candy," Chance called from his driveway, "I like the way you look today. It's amazing what a small effort can do."

"Hello, Meez Hartwell," Sancho said, grinning from ear to ear. "Thanks for giving me more chances. I like working for you."

Candy stopped and smiled into his dark eyes. "I'm the one to say thanks. I like your work and your great attitude. I think things will be okay now." She picked up some nails. "And forget the Miss Hartwell stuff, Sancho. Call me Candy."

Her thumb still seemed to be a big lump in the way so she eagerly waited for lunch time. At twelve sharp she threw down her hammer and retrieved her lunch from the car.

Chance's crew of four—five, including Judy—marched straight to the picnic tables. Her own crew followed suit. Her guys sat on one side and Chance's crew on the other. They all fit nicely at one table, but there wasn't room for Candy. She would rather be alone anyway. So, walking to the other table she sat down.

"Hey," Chance said, "we can't have this. Come on, Larry."

One of his workers jumped up and they carried the table the few feet to butt against the other one and Candy found herself sitting with the others. Chance picked up his lunch and sat across from her. Half a minute later, Judy plopped down beside him.

"Well, how do you like your work?" Candy asked.

"Great. I'm marking the sills and ceiling plates every sixteen inches to center the studs. Chance says they have to be exact and I'm doing great." She looked at him with stars shining from her big blue eyes. "Aren't I, Chance?"

He patted her knee. "You bet. You couldn't be doing better." He peeked through thick lashes at Candy.

Judy looked enraptured. "What do you like to do when you aren't working, Chance?"

He chuckled. "Well, I do lots of things. I play tennis, swim, ride horses. It's hard to say, I do so much."

Judy stuck her arm through his, completely forgetting that she was supposed to be eating and that he was trying to. "What a coincidence! Those are my favorite things to do. I can't wait to do them with you."

Since when? Candy thought. *You wouldn't know which end of a horse to feed, you're scared silly of water, and have always claimed that tennis makes you too sweaty.* She didn't say a word.

Chance had the decency to look embarrassed. "Yeah. Well, I don't seem to have much spare time right now. I usually stay out here late, cleaning up the place. Then I spend my evenings planning the next day's work and keeping the materials coming. I'm sure you see Candy doing the same things."

Judy shook her head, making her short blond curls bounce. "No, I think she leaves all that to Slade Kirkwood."

"Judy! I don't leave anything to Slade."

"She's right," Slade called grinning from his position farther down the table. "She does everthin' herself, even if it's wrong."

Soon the men drifted back to work, leaving Chance, Judy, and Candy to bring up the rear. "You'd better run, Judy," Chance said. "You know what they'll say if you can't cut it."

Judy cast an envious look at Candy and ran off to work.

Then, Chance gently pushed Candy back onto a picnic bench and sat beside her, using the table for a back rest. "You really think you can beat me with your little house?" he asked.

"Yes, I can beat you with my about-the-same-size-as-yours house."

He shrugged. "Are you ready to put your money where your mouth is?"

"What's that supposed to mean?"

"I'm ready to make a little wager. If your roof goes on first, I'll give you a hundred-dollar bill. If mine goes on first, you buy me a dinner."

Candy thought that over. Being a day or more ahead of Chance, she could hardly lose. "You're on. You haven't gained a minute on me yet. I'll just work my crew a little longer each day."

He reached his big hand out and grabbed hers, shaking it long and hard. "Okay. All set then?"

"All set. Now, if you'll give me back my hand, I better get going. I have work to do." He released her hand and she took off. Her heart sang happily and her thumb felt great. She put in a good afternoon's work.

One night, a tap on the front door interrupted the girls' gin rummy game. Dressed in her pajamas and lightweight summer robe, Candy ducked into her bedroom while Judy answered the door. Unable to believe her ears when she heard Chance's voice, she quickly got dressed, putting on her prettiest pink sundress. Then, some makeup and a quick but brisk hairbrushing prepared her to face him.

He was in an animated conversation with Judy when she came into the living room, but hearing Candy, he turned to face her. A loud wolf whistle escaped his lips.

"I could have looked beautiful, too," Judy said, "but when Candy saw who it was, she bolted for the bedroom to fix up. I had to answer the door."

"Poor baby," Chance said, eyeing her mint green shorts and tee shirt.

Candy felt anything but sorry for her little sister. That rotten kid knew how to wreck any moment. "What can we do for you this beautiful evening?" she asked, hoping he wouldn't notice her embarrassment.

"Not a thing. I finished my homework and got lonely, so here I am."

Judy jumped up. "Fantastic," she sang out. "What would you like to do? I can be ready in a minute."

Chance looked taken aback for a moment then pulled himself together. "I'd just like to relax on your comfortable couch, if you don't mind. I'm an old man, Judy, and tired, but I still crave the company of some living bodies, some real voices that might respond to something I say."

"I'll get something to drink," Candy said. She returned with tall icy lemonades to find Chance and Judy in a gin rummy game. Setting the drinks down, she turned back to the kitchen.

"Hey, where you going?" Chance asked.

"Oh, I thought I'd straighten the kitchen. You two seem to be doing all right."

"Knock." Chance laid his cards down. "Let's play something for three," he said. "You were playing when I came, weren't you?"

"Sure," Candy admitted, "but haven't you heard two's company and. . . ."

"Never. I'm going to teach you a new game, so come on."

The three spent the next two hours playing a silly game in which cheating was the object. All three laughed until they were worn out. Finally, Chance got up. "Thank you for babysitting a lonely guy tonight. You were so nice I may do it again."

"Please do," Judy chirped. "Maybe next time we can do something more exciting."

Judy barely waited for the door to swing shut before she exploded all over Candy. "You didn't really have to hang around just because he's so polite!"

"I'm sorry. I didn't realize he came to see you," Candy said.

"You what! Who did you think he came to see? You?"

Candy smiled to herself. *What does she think? I'm too old to attract a man?* She sighed. The obnoxious kid could be right. "I don't know," she said. "I thought maybe he was just lonely and wanted company."

As she lay in bed, Candy thought about the evening. She hadn't noticed Chance giving Judy a single special look—or her, for that matter. It had simply been three friends having fun together.

She had a long talk with her Heavenly Father, asking Him to help her be what He wanted her to be and to appreciate Jesus' bad day.

six

Candy worked hard trying to win the bet with Chance. One morning, all five workers scrambled to the top of the walls to receive the trusses from the crane. She hoped that by the next day at quitting time they would all be standing in place.

"I suppose you think those trusses guarantee you'll win our bet," Chance quipped at noon, popping open the clasps of his black lunch pail.

"What bet?" Judy asked, looking from one to the other, her sandwich suspended in midair.

"We're just seeing who gets a roof on first," Candy said. Hoping that would satisfy Judy, she tried to concentrate on peeling her orange.

"The woman says 'just seeing' while she puts her hand into my pocket for a hundred dollars!" Chance raised his eyebrows at Candy.

Judy looked alarmed. "Can," she almost whispered, "where will you get the one hundred dollars if you lose?"

Candy's lips tightened as she met Chance's eyes. "Don't worry. I'm not losing." She hoped he would keep his mouth shut about the rest of the bet. The last thing Judy needed was to learn about a possible dinner date between them.

A week later, while her men watched, Candy nailed on the last shake. It had been some job with the two roof levels and their being hip-roofed besides. She scampered down the ladder and ran to the street to look. The house had truly taken shape, fully worthy of her big dream.

Then her uncontrollable feet raced over to Chance's place

51

and up his ladder. "I beat you!" she squealed, flopping down on the roof beside him.

Eyes sparkling, he pulled out his billfold and removed a crisp, new hundred-dollar bill.

She reached for it but he held it back.

He pulled her close with his left hand, kissed her softly on the lips, put the bill in her hand, and released her, completing the entire maneuver before she had time to resist.

Lying back against the roof, she struggled to catch her breath.

He laughed. "That kiss was a display of sportsmanship. Wouldn't want you to think I was a sore loser."

What could she say?

"How about another wager, Candy?" he asked the next day at lunch. "The same stakes. But this time, the one who passes the framing inspection first wins."

"How can you do that? I'm farther ahead now than I was when we made the other bet. Your roof won't even be finished for two more days."

"Oh, I have my ways. Is it a bet?"

"Sure."

He grasped her hand in a hearty shake. "Did you guys hear that? If this woman takes me for another hundred I may not have enough money for payroll."

His men laughed and went to work.

Judy stood up and started to leave, then came back. "These bets aren't going to make you glad. You'd better quit before you're sad." she said petulantly. Flipping her blond curls, she stretched her long legs toward Chance's house.

Chance grinned. "Quite a girl. And quite a poet. Maybe she didn't like my display of sportsmanship."

"She doesn't know about sportsmanship. And I know you're a good sport so you won't have to show me the next time when I win."

"*If* you win. We're just getting our second wind over at my place. You won't believe what happens next."

About midafternoon, Chance came over. "Telephone for you," he said.

She ran over to answer it.

"Hello, Miss Hartwell. This is Sam Love from Century 21 Real Estate. Your check's ready for your last house. Can you sign the papers and pick it up this afternoon?"

"Can I! I'm on my way." She grabbed Chance and hugged him, then dropped her arms. "Sorry. I got carried away."

"Hey, I'm not offended. But what happened?"

"The money's ready from my last house. I have to sign the final papers."

"Great. Want some company?"

"No." She smiled, mischievously. "You'd better stay here and try to win the bet. Besides, I intend to spend the money today."

Chance whistled. "Easy come, easy go. What are you going to buy?"

Should she tell? Oh, why not? "I'm going to pay some overdue bills, temporarily save our humble home, then try to tie up those lots they're developing now. Or do you already have them in your pocket?"

"Nope. I hope you get them. Pretty soon these houses will be finished and I'd be bored to death building without any Peppermint Candy nearby."

That night, Candy couldn't contain her happiness. "What would you think about inviting Chance for supper tonight?" she asked Judy.

"Great. I'd love to. I know he's been wanting to take me out but he works too hard."

Gulp. She hadn't meant he would be Judy's date. "I just meant as a friend. I tied up five lots in the subdivision today. I'm so happy I want to celebrate."

"Don't you mean you want to rub his nose in it? I hope you plan to treat him decently."

"I do, I do. Go call, while I start supper."

Judy reappeared a little later. "He's coming. He hesitated so long I thought he wasn't going to accept. The competition between you two is ruining my chances with him."

Later, Candy heard Chance drive up and ran out to meet him as he climbed from a shiny maroon Bronco. "Neat rig. A big improvement from the beatup van you drive to work. Hey, Chance, I did it! I got the lots."

He surrounded her with a huge hug but released her almost instantly. "I'm happy for you. And me. Now we can build side-by-side for a long time. You must have made a killing on that house to buy all those expensive lots."

She shrugged. "I just put money down on them. And Judy and I'll be living on prayer until I get the next house finished and sold."

"Prayer works," said Chance. "Would you believe I've been praying for you to get those lots?"

She laughed. "I've been praying the same thing." She folded her hands and looked up. "Thank You, God," she whispered reverently.

He looked happy. "Now we can keep working together. And, speaking of God reminds me. Since you refuse to go out with me, I've been wondering if you'd go to church with me sometime."

She nodded. "I'd like that."

"Good. I'll remember." He put his arm lightly across her shoulders as they walked to the house.

When they neared the porch he stopped. "I was almost afraid to come," he said, softly. "It sounds egotistical to say out loud to anyone, and especially to you, but Judy has a crush on me."

"I've noticed."

"I guess all girls get a crush on an older man sometime in their lives, but the guy probably doesn't visit their mother."

Candy raised shocked eyes to him. Was he saying he came to see her rather than Judy? Just as she began to feel elated, she realized what he *had* said. "Hey! I may look and act it, but I'm not Judy's mother."

Judy opened the door. "Hello, Chance. Wow! Don't you look gorgeous."

Chance washed his hands and then cut up the vegetables for the salad, after which they ate like hungry construction workers.

"What would you like to do after supper?" Judy asked, when they slowed down a little.

"I'd like a rerun of my last time here. I never laughed so much in my life."

"Sounds like fun," Candy said. "I liked your crazy cheating game."

Judy's square jaw tightened a little, but she came out smiling. "Sounds like fun to me, too."

So, after they finished eating, they got right into Chance's game.

Judy put her hand on Chance's as he held his cards. "You have finger whiskers," she announced, giggling.

"Yeah?" He looked at the backs of his fingers. "Sure do. I'll shave them off the minute I get home." He moved his hands farther from Judy.

After an hour and a half of playing and laughing, Judy laid the cards on the table. "How would you like to take a walk around the block to clear the cobwebs from your brain?" she asked Chance. "You're a miserable cheater."

He raised an eyebrow. "You trying to get rid of me or something?"

"No, silly. I'm going with you."

"Well, I must not work you hard enough. Or maybe it's the elasticity of youth. Anyway, I'm going for a walk right now—to my Bronco. I'm beat."

He gathered up the cards and carefully put them back into the box. "Congratulations again, on that takeover you pulled today," he said to Candy. "In the meantime, don't forget the wager of the moment."

Candy didn't forget. She worked hard and so did her crew.

One day, she looked around. The plumber had finished, and the electrician was nearly through. Buck and Luke installed insulation where the electrician had finished, while Candy and Sancho worked on the curved stairway.

She had figured exactly how to curve it and how pie-shaped each step could safely be. When Chance appeared on the scene, the section from the front entryway to the living area was nearly finished.

He examined the stairs. "I wondered if you'd ever get around to building stairs," he said. "I almost volunteered to build them for you. Mine have been built for weeks."

Candy struggled to her feet, her knees hurting from kneeling on them so long. "I know, but yours aren't curved."

He walked up the stairs to the living level then examined the stairway a bit more. "Hey," he said, "who designed these stairs? And the round wall on the balcony? That's pretty complicated stuff."

Candy shrugged. "Me. Nothing to it if you're smart enough."

"Yeah? You and who else?"

She couldn't withhold her joy. "I really did, Chance."

A look of admiration passed over Chance's face as Slade walked up. "She'da had 'em done a long time ago if she'd asked me how," he said. Grinning at Candy, he kept going.

The next day, Candy and Sancho finished the stairway and the crew spent two more days winding up a few unfinished ends.

They were ready for inspection! Candy had won, again. She could hardly wait until lunch time. "We've done it, again," she announced as everyone started back to work. "Our house is ready for inspection. Want to pay now?"

Chance's eyes danced. "Oh, no. The bet was that the first to pass inspection wins."

"What's the big secret? Are you paying Hadleigh to flunk me? Well, he'll be here first thing in the morning. I suppose you'll be around, too?"

He nodded. "Right. I'd like to hear the excitement with my own ears. Mind?"

"Not a bit."

"Okay. See you in the morning."

Although it took forever, morning came and Henry Hadleigh arrived with his pad and pencil.

Candy met him outside. "Isn't it gorgeous?" she asked, nodding toward the house.

"It really is. You're a good learner. And this is a giant step up from the ranch styles you've been doing."

He started his inspection outside and, in a few minutes, Chance joined the procession wearing several bits of insulation in his hair. Candy wanted to take it out but resisted the impulse. The inspector ignored Chance. "Beautiful work," he said, writing furiously on his pad. "Hard to imagine this is the same outfit that, until recently, failed every inspection several times."

"Come on in. I can't wait to show you the special things I did."

They went through the basement. "I hardly need to go farther," Hadleigh said, chewing on his pencil. "Your work is all beautifully done and above code."

Chance laughed. "Oh yes, you have to do the whole house. She may have really messed up something. We want the place safe for the buyers, don't we?"

Hadleigh flushed. "I'm paid to do a job and I do it, Chancellor. By the way, in what capacity are you here?"

The right corner of Chance's lip curved. "Just a witness. Don't mind if I tag along, do you?"

Hadleigh didn't reply.

Candy twinkled at Chance. She wanted him to see her victory.

Henry Hadleigh ran up the stairs to the living area, then the bedroom level. "I've never seen anything prettier than this curved stairway and wall."

Candy and Chance joined Hadleigh on the balcony. "Now the master bedroom." She pranced in. "Are you ready for—"

But what she saw stopped her in the middle of a sentence! Shredded insulation lay over the entire floor. Electric wires had been cut, pulled from the walls, and thrown over and around the insulation, looking like long silver snakes with neither heads nor tails, but going on forever.

seven

Candy struggled to breathe. Her head felt light, the room began to spin, and she slumped to the floor. "What happened?" she finally asked in a high squeaky voice.

Hadleigh, on his knees, sifted through the debris. "Vandalism," he ground out through his teeth. "Pure unadulterated vandalism. These wires have been deliberately cut and pulled from the wall." He looked at Candy. "I'm so sorry. I realize it'll cost a lot to repair. Well, on that sad note, I'm afraid I have to leave. Dreadfully sorry."

As he clattered down the curved stairway Candy struggled to wake from her nightmare. Still feeling weak, she got to her feet. "Chance, may I use your phone to call my electrician?"

"Sure. Shall we call the police, too?"

"Yes. Call them first."

The police arrived before she returned from the disappointing call to her electrician. He could come in three days, possibly four. And where was she going to get the money to redo the work?

The officer carefully examined the destruction. "Do you have any idea who did it?" he asked when he finished.

Candy felt too crushed to think. "No," she whimpered.

The tall dark policeman scratched his nose. "About seven years ago we had a real siege of vandalism on construction."

Just what she needed. "Did you catch them?"

"No, they got tired of the game and stopped. A thing like this is hard to crack. Could be anyone."

"Did you hear the man?" Candy asked Chance after the police left. "If I want to know who did it, I have to figure it

59

out myself."

"I heard. You may as well fix it and forget it."

That night, a thought struck Candy like a meteor from the sky. Chance had had insulation in his hair! Why? Why did he tell her she would be surprised at what happened next? Because he planned to save a hundred dollars and pick up a free meal in the bargain? "Lord," she cried, "why did You let this happen? And why did You let me like him so much?" Before she fell asleep, she remembered the big man who had threatened her—Pete Meyer. He couldn't be that angry. Or could he?

The next day, her inevitable visitor stopped by as she and her crew put up the eaves' soffits. "Well, I see you're marching onward," he said.

She ignored him as she helped Sancho carry a heavy piece of plywood and lean it against the house. They returned for another.

"Look at it this way, Candy," Chance said, taking her end of the plywood. "That spiral stairway could have been chopped down."

Candy stopped short and looked at him with stark eyes. "Well, thanks for nothing. I suppose you considered it."

Chance grasped her shoulders. "What are you saying?" He looked into her eyes until she dropped her gaze to his shirt pocket. "You don't think I did it," he whispered. "Candy, you can't think that."

She glanced up at his eyes. They looked as if she had branded him with a searing iron.

"I don't know how many hundred-dollar bills you have to spare," she cried after taking a long shuddery breath. "And I don't know how much you hate the competition. You're the only person in the whole world who has anything to gain. Also, you had insulation in your hair. What can I think?"

Chance released her shoulders and put his arms around her, holding her tight. "It takes a special kind of person to do something like that. I hoped you knew by now that I'm not that kind." He put his thumb under her chin and tried to tip her face up to his, but she ducked out of his arms. "Why don't you go to church with me this weekend?" he asked. "You need to learn that if a person loves God, he couldn't do things like this.

"The Bible contains a few chapters I love so much I've memorized them. Here's part of one. Listen to it, Candy. 'Love is patient, love is kind. It does not envy, it does not boast, it is not proud. It is not rude, it is not self-seeking, it is not easily angered, it keeps no record of wrongs. Love does not delight in evil but rejoices with the truth. It always protects, always trusts, always hopes, always perseveres.' (1 Corinthians 13:4-7)

"Isn't that perfect? It tells us that if we truly love God we aren't jealous if someone has more talents or better luck or whatever. We're happy for them. We aren't happy when someone has bad luck. It's human nature to be glad when 'that guy finally gets his,' but a Christian isn't. He's on his fellow human's side. That's only the beginning of what those verses teach. If a person could just follow that one little passage, he'd be halfway to heaven already."

Tears ran down her dusty cheeks. "You're right," she said, "the verses are perfect advice. But going to church doesn't prove anything. It might even be a good cover." She pointed to his house. "Please, go. Don't you need to get ready for inspection?"

As he strode away, Candy's tears fell unchecked. Sancho, working nearby turned his back and kept very busy.

That night, Candy could hardly wait for the supper things to be cleaned up to have a talk with Judy. After they both settled in the living room to read, she casually said, "I know who vandalized the house."

Judy dropped the footrest on her recliner and sat up. "Who?"

"Chance."

Judy leaned back and put the footrest back up. "You're losing it, Can. Why would he do that?"

"To win the bet, what else? He even had insulation in his hair."

Judy dropped the footrest again and hopped out of the chair, standing tall even though leaning over. "I knew that bet would cause trouble," she yelled down at Candy. Then, her look softened and her voice became pleading. "He's been helping to insulate his house, Can. That's why he had the stuff in his hair. I hope you didn't tell him your crazy idea."

"Yep. I sure did."

"Can! Don't you realize what you're doing to me?"

Candy climbed out of her chair, too, and stood to her full height—looking up six more inches to Judy. "You just tell me one other person who would do such a thing. Just one!"

Judy leaned down until her forehead touched Candy's. "What about that guy you told me about? The one who got so mad at you. But, I don't think it was him, either. Your house simply happened to be in the wrong place at the wrong time."

"What about the note? I suppose they aren't connected?"

"I'm not sure. But, I know about Chance. Chance is noble, Chance is true. He only does what God would want him to do."

Candy went to bed wishing for Judy's faith. "Dear Father," she pleaded, "help me know if it was him. I'm really dumb, so show me for certain, okay? Thank You, Lord, in Jesus' name. Amen." Relaxing quietly, all the things Chance had done to help her popped into her head. And the considerate way he treated his men. Frequently, she wakened and repeated the same prayer with the same results each time. By morning, she felt a deep peace and knew Chance didn't do it. She couldn't wait to tell Judy that God had answered her prayers, and she did so at breakfast.

"Good," Judy said, spreading strawberry jam on her toast. "I'm glad we got that settled." She took a big juicy bite, chewed it, and swallowed noisily. "But you don't have to be a genius to figure out he'd never do anything like that."

When Candy arrived at work, she went looking for Chance to tell him of her prayer experience. As she wandered through his house, doubts began to slither back into her mind. Maybe she had been dreaming last night when she had thought God had answered her prayers. How was she supposed to know? A memory verse she had learned as a child popped into her mind. *God is not a man that He should lie, nor a son of man, that he should change his mind.* (Numbers 23:19) Well, that surely meant she could always trust what He said—without letting doubts wreck her faith.

Then, she remembered she owed Chance a dinner. She would pay off her bet and forget about it. Chance's foreman met her and told her Chance wouldn't be at work today. "Do you know why he isn't here?" she asked.

"Said he wasn't feeling well but I've been with him for ten years and it's the first time he's ever been sick."

"Well, everyone has a right to be sick once in ten years. Thanks, Johnny."

Candy went back to work feeling guilty. As time passed, the

feeling intensified. Finally, she asked Johnny for Chance's home address.

Using the hose, she washed her face and arms, then readjusted the car's rearview mirror to brush her hair and put on a little makeup. Now, one more stop—the florist.

A few minutes later, Candy pulled to the side of the road, checked the name on the mailbox, and drove down the long paved driveway to the immense modern-looking house.

A middle-aged Asian woman opened the door. Candy swallowed hard and switched the tiny bouquet into her other hand. "I'd like to see Mr. Chancellor, please?"

"Follow me," the woman said.

Candy followed the woman through a monstrous living room with white leather furniture, up wide stairs, down a hall. Finally, the woman stopped beside a doorway and motioned Candy in.

Candy stepped through the door and found herself in a large office overlooking an expanse of green lawn resembling that in front of the house, except that an Olympic-sized swimming pool stood in the middle. Large weeping willows and maples bordered the pool making it a shady oasis. Beyond the lawn, several horses grazed; a red barn stood behind the pasture.

Candy took her eyes from the lovely scene to discover Chance sitting at a drafting table to the left. His red-rimmed eyes met hers then dropped back to his drawing.

"Hi," Candy sang out, handing him the flowers. "Whatever is wrong?"

"Oh, just an allergy. But I'm using the time to design my next house."

"When am I paying my debt? Your house will pass for sure."

"Want to sit down?" He pointed to a woven chair.

"Sure. Will you be well enough tonight?" Candy asked.

"I can't accept any payment. You were ready for inspection before I. And your house was okay. I lost." Chance's voice held none of its usual vibrancy. He pulled a hundred-dollar bill from his wallet and offered it to her.

"Put that thing away. I lost—and I pay. The question is when?"

He struggled to his feet and pulled her from the rocker. "Do you still think I was behind that mess?" he asked.

She hesitated, then laughed. "I've forgotten all about it."

He dropped her hands as if they were hot. "I'll mail you a check for the hundred if you won't take the bill."

She had hurt him again. "Chance," she cried, "I know you didn't do it. God even showed me. I can't handle having you feel bad."

He stood up. "Thanks for the flowers, Candy. I really appreciate them." Taking her elbow, he steered her out of the room and down the stairs. Then, she stood alone on the porch looking at the closed door.

"Did you know Chance was sick today?" Judy asked as Candy stepped through the front door that evening. "Johnny says he's sick of being accused of things he didn't do."

Candy didn't feel like getting into anything with Judy. "I know," she said gently. "I took him some flowers."

Judy's mouth dropped open but she said nothing. She moved into the kitchen and Candy followed.

"Yep," Candy said, "he's okay."

Judy got her voice back. "You owe him an apology." She pulled a meatloaf from the oven. Putting a baked potato onto each plate and a salad on the table, Judy plopped into her chair, still glaring at Candy.

The girls ate in silence. Later as they watched television, Candy mulled over what Judy had said. She would apologize tomorrow. Not that an apology would fix everything.

In her private devotions that night, Candy prayed for the Lord to renew her faith. And in her reading she found a verse that made her feel totally unsaved. *For in the gospel a righteousness from God is revealed, a righteousness that is by faith from first to last, just as it is written: "The righteous will live by faith."* (Romans 1:17)

She crawled into bed thinking about the verse. Where had her strong faith gone? Did she have even enough left to accept Christ's sacrifice for her anymore?

The next day, Chance came to work and sat across from her at noon.

Judy plopped down beside him. "You look awful," she said. "What was wrong, anyway?"

He looked uncomfortable. "Just a little allergy."

"Come again, Chancellor," Johnny yelled from the other end of the table. "You've never had an allergy in your life."

Chance shoved a sandwich into his mouth and said nothing.

"Can I do anything to make you more comfortable?" Judy asked.

Chance's laugh sounded forced. "I'm all right. Enough about my illness."

Candy waited until the crews returned to work. "I have a wonderful idea how I can pay my debt to you," she said. "Does it have to be a meal in a restaurant?"

His lips lay in a tight, straight line; the muscles in his neck jumped spasmodically. "It doesn't have to be a meal anywhere. I don't want to hear anymore about it."

"Okay," she continued, "can you make it next Saturday? I'm packing a picnic lunch and driving up into the mountains."

He said nothing.

Candy went around to his side of the table and massaged his shoulders. "I'm sorry I hurt you, Chance. I'd give anything to be able to take back my words, but they're gone. The Lord showed me you didn't do it. He also showed me what a special person you are and I believed Him. Then, right away, doubts began to creep back into my mind. God has been bringing me some powerful Bible verses but pretty soon I doubt them, too. I was bragging how my faith could never fail—and all that kind of stuff. Now it's gone and I don't know what to do about it. Won't you please forgive me?"

He sat quietly a moment, then smiled thinly. "Okay, what time does the bus leave?"

Candy continued the massage, all smiles. "Any time after nine o'clock."

She finished and walked around the table. "I have to get to work now, if I hope to win the next bet." She turned and hurried away.

"Candy, wait."

She returned.

"No more bets," he said.

"Okay, no more bets. Now, am I dismissed?"

"Yeah. Get out of here."

As Candy worked, she wondered how Judy would take it when she learned about the excursion to the mountains. She could hardly sneak off for the entire day. Hurrying through the house, she noticed the master bedroom repair was coming along nicely. The sheetrockers were, too.

"I'm going out tonight, Can," Judy said on Friday night. "I've been waiting for Chance but he won't call this weekend because he isn't well yet."

What luck! Candy had to fix the picnic lunch. "That's great, Judy," she said. "Who are you going with?"

"Victor Price. He's nice, but just a kid."

Candy smiled. "What do you think you are? I'm glad to see you having fun."

"Well, it'll be something to do. Vic's been asking me for months, so I decided, why not?"

"Right. Why not? So go make yourself even prettier than usual."

An hour later, when Vic's car disappeared, Candy smiled. Vic did look young, but what wonderfully clean good looks.

Then she flew into the kitchen where she fried a chicken, made potato salad, jello salad, and a small torte. After everything was tucked safely into the refrigerator she went to the store and bought a small watermelon and a six-pack of soda. She had to watch her pennies even on special occasions. Back home, she tucked the watermelon and pop into the refrigerator to cool overnight along with the chicken and salads. Then, she eagerly pulled out the new novel she had bought from the Christian bookstore.

It seemed only minutes before laughter jerked her from the story and Judy and Vic tumbled into the living room.

"Don't pay any attention to us, Can." Judy took Vic's hand and led him toward the kitchen. "We're starved," she called as they disappeared through the door.

When Candy heard the refrigerator door open, she scrunched down in her chair. They would find the picnic lunch for sure.

As Candy tried to decide how to tell Judy, the two young

people came back into the living room. Judy had a plateful of chicken, potato salad, beans, and a slice of toast. Vic had two plates identical to Judy's. He handed one to Candy and sat on the couch.

"Hey, thanks, Can," Judy said. "This is great."

"Yeah," Vic said. "It really hits the spot."

Candy crunched into her chicken breast. Who could tell the truth after all that? She would fix another lunch in the morning.

The alarm seemed to go off only moments after she dropped to her pillow. Reaching over to turn it off, she remembered that she and Chance were going to the mountains and she immediately came wide awake. She jumped out of bed, into the shower, then to the kitchen.

Just as she feared, the potato salad and all the good pieces of chicken were completely gone. She grinned, wondering what Chance would say if she took wings, neck, gizzard, and backs. Oh well, she would substitute cold cuts.

Fifteen minutes later, she drank a cup of coffee while the potatoes and eggs cooled in the freezer. This could be a fantastic day—if Chance had forgiven her.

And how did she really feel about the vandalism? Was it just a random hit? Or did someone do it especially to her? A random hit was a little hard to believe, considering the note. But she could forgive Chance. *Wait a minute! She knew Chance didn't do it. Didn't she? No, she didn't know anything. But God had shown her, really shown her that Chance would never do a thing like that. A tear dripped from her left eye as she wondered if she had any faith at all.*

As she sat meditating, Judy stumbled in, tousled, un-combed, with sleep in her eyes. "Hi. How come you're up so early, Can?"

Well, this was it. "Good morning, Judy." She poured a steaming cup of coffee and handed it to the younger girl. "It's hot. Now, why am I up? Well, Chance and I are going up into the Blues today to help him feel better, sort of make up for causing him to get sick in the first place you know."

Judy gasped and spun around, took two steps back and faced Candy like an injured animal.

"Judy, don't look like that. Everything's all right. Chance and I are just going to have a boring day relaxing. I thought you'd want me to make it up to him."

Judy's dilated pupils and flaring nostrils screamed silently at Candy. She had never seen her little sister so upset. Judy leaned forward, her hands clenched into tight fists. Breathing hard, she glared at Candy a moment then bolted for her room.

Candy finished the potato salad and put it into the ice chest. Putting the rest of the lunch together, she loaded it into the car then tapped on Judy's door. No response, only quiet sobbing. After tapping again, Candy went in and sat on the bed. "Why do you feel so bad?" she asked softly.

Judy sat up, her wide, tear-stained eyes on Candy's. "You don't even like him. You've barely ever said a decent word about him. So why can't you let me have him?"

"Oh, baby, I do like him. And he's twelve years older than you. Vic is so much nicer for you."

"Vic's a kid. And you don't like Chance, Can. You're just trying to hurt me. Why?"

eight

"Judy, the last thing I want to do is fight with you over a guy. So why don't you wash your face and come along. There's plenty of—"

"Hey, anyone home?" Chance called from the living room.

"You go fix up pretty. We'll wait."

Candy hurried out to Chance. "Sit down, quick. I have something to tell you." She pushed him onto the couch and dropped down beside him. "Hey, what happened to your thumb?"

He glanced at the bloody bandage and shrugged. "I dropped a glass in the sink, then cut my thumb picking the pieces out of the strainer."

"Is it all right?" she asked.

He nodded.

"Okay, then listen. Judy just found out we're going and feels so awful I had to invite her to come. I hope you don't mind. There's plenty of food."

"I do mind. A lot." He took Candy's other hand then grinned. "I was counting on this being just us. I had all kinds of ideas where this day might lead."

Candy felt elated but forced herself to continue. "One more thing. Judy accused me of trying to take you away from her, so we can't do anything together anymore until she understands you two are either on or off."

He dropped her hand. "How am I supposed to do that?"

She smiled impishly. "That's your problem. I think you can handle it. But not today, please. By the way, what are you doing here? Wasn't I supposed to pick you up?"

"I figured if my car were here, you'd have a harder time getting rid of me tonight. Right?"

She thought a moment, then laughed. "Right. I could have taken you home and dumped you."

As she lifted her hand to knock on the bedroom door, Judy stepped out in pastel blue shorts and top. Her big blue eyes looked a bit sad, but her wide smile belied the fact.

Suddenly, the telephone rang. As Candy returned to the living room, Chance beat her to the shrilling telephone. He stood facing her, with his back to the phone. "Don't answer," he pleaded. "Someone's trying to wreck our day."

"Don't be silly." She laughed and tried to push him out of the way. "What could happen? All the important people are right here."

He remained nailed to the floor.

"Move aside." She gave a giant shove and grabbed the phone, only to receive the dial tone.

"Now look what you did. No matter, let's go."

After she started the car, she ran back to the house to check the doors. Once again the phone rang. This time she got it on the third ring.

"Miss Hartwell?"

"Yes."

"Hugh Perry, Mountain View Police Department. Are you building a new home on Paradise Heights?"

Ice gathered around her heart. "Yes, I am."

"Why don't you run over to the house? We'd like to talk to you."

"I'm on my way." Candy dumped the phone and ran out the door, locking it behind her.

Jumping into the car, she said nothing until her car flowed with the traffic. "The call you interrupted was from the police."

Chance's lips formed a hard line and the cords in his neck stood out. "What's wrong now?"

She made a left turn, her lips trembling. "Probably burned to the ground."

"Don't borrow trouble. Maybe you broke a law or something."

"Sure."

Silence filled the car until they reached the new subdivision and pulled up to the house. Two police cars sat at the curb and four officers walked around the house. WOMAN GO HOME! had been spray-painted in huge red letters over the entire front side of her unpainted house.

Candy slumped over the steering wheel. This was definitely the same person who had written the note.

Chance sat a moment then gathered her into his arms. "It won't take an hour to paint over that. I'll help you on Monday."

She nestled against his shoulder and sobbed. "It isn't the work, it's the message. Don't you see? Someone doesn't want me building."

He brushed a dark curl away from her face. "Who cares? We won't let them chase you out. We'll. . . ."

A police officer approached the car. "Miss Hartwell," he said, "you'd better come talk with us."

Candy pulled a tissue from her purse, wiped her eyes, and blew her nose. Then, she followed the policeman, with Chance and Judy walking quietly behind.

When they rounded the corner, the officer pointed to the back of the house where the fifteen-foot picture window had been broken out, leaving shards of glass around the edges. Candy caught her breath. She wouldn't cry again.

"I'm sorry," the officer said, steering her to the other end of the house where the eight-foot sliding glass door had been smashed.

Candy ran to the picnic table and sat down. The officer, then Chance and Judy, followed. "Is there more?" Candy asked.

"As far as we know, that's all, but there's a lot of money in that broken glass, Miss Hartwell."

"Tell me about it," Candy said, then cradled her head on her curved arms on the picnic table.

Chance got up. "I'm going to look around inside." Judy followed.

"We looked inside," the officer said. "I think this is it—for now. You've had vandalism before. Since no one else has been bothered, we believe it's someone who feels you're out of place trying to build. Or can you think of anything personal?"

Candy sniffed. And thought. "No." She wiped her nose. "I haven't bothered anyone."

"We'll send extra patrols into the neighborhood now."

Chance and Judy came out of the house. "It's all right inside, Can," Judy said. "Not even any glass."

"Yeah," Chance said grimly. "That means the windows were broken from the inside. Candy, your exterior doors are on. Why weren't they locked?"

"I thought they were."

"Well, they're locked now. And they'd better always be. Hear?"

"I hear."

"Well, what are we going to do now?" Judy asked, checking her face in her small compact mirror.

"We're going into the mountains," Chance said. "Hit the car, mates."

Candy lifted distressed eyes. "I don't feel like going anymore."

"What do you want to do?" Chance asked. "Sit home and feel sorry for yourself? No way. I'll make one condescension. I'll drive." He winked at her. "Been dying to drive this thing, anyway."

"Okay," Candy agreed, "I'll ride in the back for a while." Chance held the door open while she scooted through to the back seat. Judy eagerly accepted the invitation to ride in front with him.

Candy fixed herself a makeshift bed, using the folded quilt for a pillow, and relaxed.

"We couldn't ask for nicer weather," Chance said to Judy. "The sky's still a deep blue."

"Not as blue as your eyes," she returned.

"My eyes aren't very blue anymore. Did you know that as people get older their eyes lose their color?"

She gave him a small shove. "You're putting me on. You have the bluest eyes I've ever seen."

Candy could almost hear Chance's gears turning, looking for a safe topic to discuss. Then, "Are you taking college prep classes, Judy? I barely remember my college days it's been so long."

"It has not. Yes, Can's been making me prepare for college, but I may not go. Candy didn't, you know. I may not even finish high school. I'd just as soon work for you. What can I learn in college that'll pay more?"

He glanced at her. "Whoa. I don't build much in the winter. My crew will be cut down to one other guy and me. Know where that leaves you?"

"You still can't make me go to college."

"Think about all the nice guys you'll meet."

"I don't want to meet guys."

Candy saw a cord in Chance's neck tighten. What would he do next? But she felt the car slowing to a stop. Sitting up, she discovered a pretty little lake on her right.

They hopped out and ran to the water. Judy pulled off her outer clothes first, wearing a two-piece bathing suit underneath. Candy followed, wearing a modest one-piece red suit. Both stepped into the icy lake and turned to Chance who stood on the bank with his hands in his pockets.

"Hey," Candy yelled, shivering. "Come on in. It's warm as toast."

"I better not," he said. "My rheumatism's been acting up a lot lately."

What's he doing? Candy wondered. *He loves to swim.* Then she noticed his bloody bandage. His cut thumb! He had admitted to cutting it on glass, but could it have been window glass? Of course he hadn't cut it on window glass! She shoved the thought from her mind.

Judy splashed back to shore and scampered up beside him. "Get rid of your clothes or I'm going to shove you in with them on. You do have a swimsuit on, don't you?"

"Yes, but I'd forgotten how cold these mountain lakes are. I probably wouldn't be able to work for a week if I did. I'm not so young as I used to be."

Judy gave him a funny look and jumped in. It took only a few minutes for the mountain water to chill the girls, so they climbed up on the rock beside Chance and rested in the sun while they dried.

"When do we eat?" Judy asked.

"Let's go on to the next lake," Chance suggested.

He winked at Candy as he settled her gently into the seat beside him. "How are you now?"

"Oh, I guess I'll live. That is if the vandal doesn't decide to work on me directly."

He shuddered, then started the car and pulled onto the road. "Don't even make jokes like that. It isn't funny."

As they continued climbing, another little blue lake sparkled to their right. "Here's a good place," Chance said, pulling into a parking space.

When they sat down to the delicious meal, Chance groaned. "I'm afraid the food's too spicy for me. I know I can't eat the potato salad. It might set my gallbladder off. Maybe I could eat some of the blander cold cuts with bread."

Judy looked at him with shocked eyes but filled her plate heaping full.

Candy knew he was doing something, but what? He had a stomach like a gravel crusher and nothing short of dynamite could set his gallbladder off. She filled her plate and said nothing.

He fixed a sandwich of roast beef and bread—with nothing on it. Refusing pop and cake, he ate a small slice of watermelon.

Finally, late in the afternoon the little blue car took them home. After they unloaded the picnic things, Chance turned to Candy. "Could I leave my car here tonight?" he asked in a pitifully weak voice. "I feel too tired to drive. Maybe you could drive me home."

She drove several blocks waiting for him to explain. He didn't. "Okay, wise guy," she finally said. "What's up?"

Chance shrugged. "Nothing's up. In fact, I thought I seemed sort of on the down side. Did you notice how terribly much too old I am for Judy? That kid can do anything and eat everything."

Candy burst into laughter. "I did notice how terribly old

you are."

Chance laughed, too. "Can you steer this thing to a restaurant of some sort?" he asked, rubbing his stomach. "I'm starved."

Candy pulled into a taco shop where Chance ordered soda and six tacos and didn't look up until he had four down. Candy ordered two.

When they arrived at his place, he jerked the key from the ignition and pulled her into his arms. "Thanks for a fantastic day," he said. "Can you go out with me now once in a while?"

"I'd love to," Candy said, swallowing all thoughts about his cut thumb. "But it depends on Judy. How about going to your church in the morning?"

His smile lit up Candy's heart. "You got it. Does Judy go too?"

Candy shook her head. "I'm not sure. But I'd better get home before she comes looking for me."

He kissed her tenderly. Bells rang and fireworks burned through her brain. She drove home on a pink cloud.

When Candy walked through the door, Judy's eyes flashed. "What have you been doing all this time? Didn't you know I was waiting—and worrying about Chance?"

"He wanted something to eat so I got it for him," Candy said. "That's all there was to it."

"You know what I think, Can? I think you're falling for him. Remember, I liked him while you hated him."

"Oh, Judy, haven't you noticed how much older he is than you? He's even older than I thought. After today I wonder if he's too old for me." Candy sighed and rested her head on the back of the couch. "Do you have any ideas who could be destroying my house?"

"How would I know? And why should I care?"

"Oh," Candy said gently, "you care because you love me and don't want anyone to hurt me. Which, incidentally, hurts you, too."

"I don't care. You're hurting me." Judy jumped off the couch and slammed into her bedroom. But, the next morning, she recovered sufficiently to go to church with Chance and Candy.

Chance, in a dark suit, nearly took Candy's breath away. But, in spite of the heart-rending music, she didn't like his big church as well as her small one. The minister's stirring presentation of Christ's sacrifice made her fall in love with her Lord all over again. She went home full of faith and determined to keep it strong.

When Candy arrived at work Monday morning her men all stood in the front yard reading the garish message on the house. Sancho met her. "Meez Hartwell. . . . I mean Candy, don't read it. It's not nice."

Candy noticed the other three men all watching her intently. "It's all right, Sancho," she said, "I've already read it. Have you seen the back of the house?"

"No, Meez . . . Candy. More nasty signs?"

"They used more than words in the back," Candy said softly. "They broke the big windows."

Sancho took off running around the house. The others followed, including Candy. They stopped behind the living room and looked up toward the window.

"What . . . ?" Buck said. "When did all this happen?"

"Friday night. The police called Saturday. Rotten, isn't it?"

"Yes," Luke said, "real rotten. It's time to put a stop to this foolishness. The police better put a nightly guard on it."

"Great idea," Candy said, nodding, "but I don't think they

do that on private property."

"Then let's take turns watching," Buck said. "I'd like to catch the low-life who'd do this to a woman."

"Yeah," Luke said, "It won't be too good for him if I catch him."

"I really appreciate you guys," Candy said, "but I'm going to be hard-pressed to get the house finished with these extra expenses. I won't be able to pay for all that extra time."

"Who's talking pay?" Buck said. "We're in this together, aren't we?"

"Yeah," Luke agreed.

Slade held up his hand. "Hold it. I know you guys got good hearts, but you ain't thought this here thing through very good. Someone could get hurt."

Sancho had been gathering glass and putting it in a large cardboard box. He approached Candy, all smiles. "I peek it all up, Meez Candy. Now anybody won't get feet or hands cut."

"Thanks, Sancho. You're the greatest." The little man walked back to the house looking as if she had given him a hundred dollars.

"We'll build the bedroom balcony and living room deck today," she said. "The redwood will be here in a few minutes." As the men scurried away, Candy wondered how she could pay for the enormous windows twice.

nine

"Your guys were telling me they want to take turns watching the place, Candy," Chance said as the crews ate lunch. "I'll take my turn. We can put a stop to this if we work together."

"I spent first night," Sancho said. "I bring my sleeping bag. I spent every night, you want."

Chance patted the little man on the shoulder. "No reason for you to do it all, Sancho. We'll take turns. I'll take the second night. I have an old cot I'll set up."

Buck spoke for the third night and Luke took fourth.

Chance turned to Slade. "How about you, Kirkwood?"

Slade lit a cigarette and inhaled deeply. "I suppose I'll take the fifth day. But we won't never catch anyone."

"We sure won't if we don't try," Chance said, lips taut and voice crisp. Then he grinned at Candy. "Candy'll pick up each of you just before dark and leave you here so there'll be no car."

"Yes. I'll do that," Candy said. "And I hope it isn't dumb. I wouldn't want anyone hurt. Hey, we'd better eat lunch."

"No one's going to get hurt," Chance said, unwrapping a small pack of cookies. "This guy's too much of a yellow-belly to be dangerous."

"Okay, we may as well get to work," Candy said ten minutes later. "The only way this house will ever get finished is sticking to it."

That night, Victor Price arrived looking for Judy. Candy didn't ask where they were going; frankly she didn't care. Vic was a nice boy, just right for taming her wild little sister.

Just before dusk, she picked up Sancho at the trailer he had

81

appropriated and took him to the house. "Are you afraid?" she asked.

"Oh, no, Meez Candy. This—what you say—yellow-belly don't scare me."

"Will you be comfortable on the cot?"

"Better than trailer."

"Okay," Candy said with a wave, "I'll see you in the morning."

Judy arrived home soon after Candy. "It really was fun being with a young guy," she said, pouring root beers for both of them.

Candy put three ice cubes in each glass and the girls sat down at the kitchen table. "What did you do?"

"We did all the things old people can't do. Swam at The Splash, ate greasy food, too. Can you imagine Chance going down those mile-long slides, Can?"

Candy took a long drink . . . and smiled. She couldn't imagine Judy going down, either. Maybe discovering how *old* Chance is made Judy appreciate her youth a little more. Anyway, they'd done all the things Chance couldn't do because of his advanced age.

"I'm happy for you," Candy said, meaning every word. She wisely didn't mention her thought that if Judy were thinking about Vic, she would probably forget Chance.

When Candy arrived the next morning with his breakfast, Sancho looked rested. "I sleep like the dead, Meez Candy. No one come near."

That day at lunch, Judy sat at the other end of the table. Candy tried not to watch her little sister but couldn't help noticing how she and one of Chance's men, Larry, couldn't seem to get close enough to each other.

That night, Candy planned to pick up Chance at his place, but he showed up at her house. "Thought we could talk a bit," he explained, patting the couch beside him.

She sat down. "Anything special?"

"I just wanted to be with you a while before the lonely night."

She glanced at him and smiled. "Poor baby. Now let me see . . . who pushed this surveillance thing? Not that I don't appreciate it."

He reached his arm around her and pulled her to him—and the doorbell chimed.

After Candy introduced Vic and Chance, they visited until Judy came down and the young people left.

"Nice kid," Chance said.

Candy nodded agreement. "Judy told me about their last night out. You'll appreciate it. They swam—at that wild place—then ate greasy food. She remarked how nice it was to be with someone young enough to enjoy those things."

Chance laughed. "You mean that little trick worked?" He reached for Candy again and pulled her close. "But, how do you feel about old men?"

"I don't have anything against old men. In fact, it's time to take one to do his guard duty."

"I'll bring your breakfast in the morning," Candy said when they reached the house. "Mine, too. Those picnic tables have been great."

Chance unlocked the door and they stepped into the nearly dark house. "I put those tables there to ease your mind about Judy."

"I know. Thanks. And now, I have a question. What do you know about your man, Larry?"

"Larry Grant?" He shook his head. "He's twenty-three.

Hey, you aren't eyeing him, are you?"

Candy laughed. "Hardly. But I noticed he and Judy looked pretty cozy at lunch today."

Chance shook his head again. "He came along in the spring looking for a job." He shrugged. "He's a good worker."

"What if she decides to go somewhere with him?"

"Maybe she won't. After all she has Vic."

After a while Candy got up to leave and pecked his cheek. He jumped up, engulfed her in his arms, and kissed her with passion.

Whoa! Candy's legs felt weak so she hung on.

He smiled as he steadied her. "Got you, too, huh?" He kissed her again, more gently.

That night, Candy again asked the Lord if Chance was what he claimed to be. The peace that soothed her heart told her He had answered. She also asked Him to stop the vandalism and to watch over Judy. She had a hard time falling asleep though, hoping Chance wouldn't get hurt. She giggled. At least if he got hurt she would know for sure he wasn't the villain. She jerked herself into a sitting position. How could she even wonder about Chance when God had answered her prayer so plainly, less than five minutes ago? That must be a record, even for her, in faithlessness.

The next morning, Chance met her at the picnic table ready for breakfast. As they ate, Candy decided to believe God's assurance completely and enjoy Chance's friendship.

At lunch that day everyone seemed in unusually high spirits. Maybe because nothing had happened to the house for a couple of days. Judy sat with Larry again and the two seemed to know each other well. Candy shook her head, pushing away a darkness that threatened her feeling of well-being.

"I think I'll stay in the house every night," Chance said, reaching for another of Candy's sandwiches. "I eat better than when I make my own food."

"I stay too," Sancho agreed. "Meez Candy make great food."

"I can't, really," Chance said. "I have to be out of town for a few days. But I'll be ready to have a turn when I get back."

Candy felt a rock land in her stomach and hop into her throat. She laid her cookie on the table, unable to swallow.

"I guess it's my turn tonight, isn't it?" Buck asked. "That's what this thing's turning out to be. A time to eat Candy's food."

Nothing happened that night while Buck watched, nor the next night while Luke did. The next night, Friday, Slade grudgingly agreed to stay.

When Candy got home from delivering him to the house, she found Judy waiting for her. "Larry and I are going into the mountains tomorrow," she announced "What can I take?"

"You aren't going into the mountains with Larry," Candy said. "What do you know about him?"

Judy's eyes flashed and her hands clenched into fists. "Enough to go with him. I suppose he's a jerk like Chance? At least you can't say he's too old."

"Oh yes, I can. You should be going with a teenager. How about inviting him here so I can meet him?"

Judy shook her head. "He doesn't like mothers. I'm going with him, Can, whether you like it or not."

"You are *not* going with him, Judy. End of discussion." Candy stormed into the living room and snatched up the newspaper, hoping she had been strong enough to convince her stubborn little sister.

A half hour later, Judy crept in and sat in the rocker across from the couch. "We decided we'd just do something around town tomorrow," she said, softly.

Candy didn't know whether to be thankful for the small victory or insist Judy not go with the guy at all. "What do you have in mind?" she asked. "Could you just make it an afternoon date? I'd be glad to cook a nice meal for you both later. Then I'd disappear into my bedroom."

Judy made a face. "I'll make it an afternoon date but he isn't about to ask permission to take me out. Can, he's twenty-three."

Candy had to smile. "I know. Way too old for a teenager. But let's forget him for now. I have something serious to talk about. Okay?"

Judy looked fearful. "Did I do something else?"

Candy pulled her down onto the couch beside her. "No. I'm just wondering how I'm going to finish the house. I've had to redo so much that I'll run out of money before it's finished. I can't sell the house until it's finished, and I don't have any more money."

"I see." Judy propped her feet on the coffee table and studied her pink socks a moment. "You can't sell it until it's finished and you can't finish it until you sell it. What a pain! If I had money I'd lend it to you."

Candy lifted appreciative eyes to the younger woman. "I know you would. Thanks for the thought."

Judy crossed her feet. "You can use all the money Chance pays me. I don't need it."

Candy swallowed. "You need that worse than I do, Judy, but thanks anyway." She didn't mention how pitiful Judy's paycheck would look against the debts.

Candy sat staring blankly, seeing a mountain of

construction bills. She would soon be facing tough collection agencies. Did they put people in jail for not paying their bills?

After reading a chapter in her Bible, she fell asleep praying for God to watch over Judy and also her house.

The next morning, Candy tried to pretend Judy wasn't going anywhere, but a little after noon, Larry Grant drove up in his old pickup and honked until Judy ran out.

"Be back by seven o'clock," Candy called as she waved goodbye.

Judy waved and jumped into the slowly moving vehicle.

Candy felt bored and lonely with both Judy and Chance gone. Not that she would have seen him anyway, but knowing he was out of town made her miss him.

Seven o'clock passed with no sign of Judy. The clock hands passed eight, ten, twelve, and two. Candy didn't know whether to be furious or frightened. When three o'clock passed, she suddenly had to call the police! She had punched out three numbers when Larry's pickup screamed down the street and screeched to a halt. A moment later, Judy opened the door.

"Where have you been?" Candy asked, louder than necessary.

"Out." Judy hurried toward her bedroom.

Candy jumped in front of her. "I want to know what you've been doing and I want to know now!"

Judy pushed her aside and ran into her bedroom. "I didn't go to the mountains. That's what you wanted, wasn't it?" She shut the door quietly and the lock clicked into place.

ten

"Judy, you open this door right now!" Candy yelled through the door. No response. "I was calling the cops when you came home and if you don't open the door I'll call them now. I have to know what happened to you!"

After a moment, the lock clicked and the door slowly opened. "Why do you have to get so excited?" Judy asked.

"Because I don't know what he did to you. Tell me right now."

Judy laughed. "He didn't do anything to me. That should fill your heart with glee."

"What have you been doing all this time then?"

Judy started to turn back to her room but shook her head and sat on the rocker. "I suppose you have to know it all. First, we went to the park and fed the ducks. Then we went to a movie, then we went to Walla Walla and got hamburgers and came back. After that, we went to another movie, then had milk shakes." She grinned. "That's it, Mom."

"I guess that's all right, but staying out eight hours too long isn't. You'll have to be punished, Judy."

Judy laughed. "Okay. I'm knee-knocking scared. Good night." A moment later the lock clicked again.

Candy dropped into her bed at four-fifteen in the morning.

The next morning, unable to awaken Judy, Candy went to church alone. Driving home, she thanked God for her blessing. She needed to feel close to Him after last night's scare.

Monday morning seemed lonely to Candy even with her crew there. "Hey, Johnny," she called at lunch, "when's

Chance coming back?"

"Any time."

"Are we staying in the house this week?" Sancho asked, changing the subject.

"It ain't necessary," Slade said. "Everything's stayin' in one piece now."

"Nothing happened last week when we were here," Buck said. "I'd rather sleep in my own bed."

The flooring arrived and Candy showed the truck driver where to put it. Later, as Candy squatted while painting the balcony rails, she felt herself grasped by the shoulders and pulled over backwards, onto her behind—and Chance's laughing face appeared above her. Dropping the paint brush, she threw her arms around him, getting only a little paint on him.

He held her at arm's length. "Hey, I'm going away more often. I do believe you missed me."

"I missed you, I missed you, I missed you."

Soon, he went to check on his own house and men.

Candy went back to work, singing happily. He didn't have to be right here. Just having him over at his own place took away all her loneliness.

Before she left that afternoon, Chance returned. "How would you like to go out for bowling and pizza with Judy and her guy tonight?" he asked.

"Sure. What time?"

"I have to be here a while longer. How about seven-thirty?"

Had she ever been this happy? "I'll be ready."

Candy had a good evening bowling, seeming unable to miss.

Back home, Candy and Chance sat at the kitchen table while Vic and Judy watched television in the living room. "You did a lot of work while I was gone," Chance said, holding Candy's hand on the table top.

"We worked hard, but your house is going to be finished first. No doubt about that now."

"Of course. I have to finish my house first so I can snatch the buyer that would have bought yours."

Candy saw caring love in his eyes, and felt answering emotions. She had never met a man like Chance.

Needing to think about something else, she told him about Judy's long night out with Larry, her fear and worry. "Can you make them stop seeing each other?"

He shook his head. "You're the one that should do that. But have they done anything so awful?"

"Yes! Getting home eight hours late is a major offense. I was calling the cops when they got home. I let Judy know how I felt, too."

He caressed her hand. "Why don't you give them another chance? Maybe Judy will be more careful now. Have a little faith in her."

After Chance left, Candy thought about the faith business. She definitely lacked faith, but did it have to encompass her whole entire life? Faith in God, faith in Chance. Maybe she *should* try to generate some faith in Judy since she couldn't control her anymore. *Help me, Father. I seem to be lacking in every department. Show me how to have faith.* Almost immediately, she knew that first she had to have faith in God, then faith in others would follow.

Then a verse popped into her mind. *Consequently, faith comes from hearing the message, and the message is heard through the word of Christ.* (Romans 10:17) Well, did she need to spend more time reading the Bible? She could do that. In fact, she wouldn't mind that at all. She had already been reading a chapter each night. Now, she would start to read two each night. She would drop Isaiah and start the Gospels—that's where she would find the words of Christ.

Then she thought about the house she was building—or trying to build. That's what wrecked her faith. If she had enough money to finish it she would feel able to handle her other problems, even Judy.

She read the first two chapters of Matthew; they were mostly background. When she got into Jesus' grown-up years, she hoped it would increase her faith.

The next morning, when Candy stepped inside the new house, she heard people talking in hushed voices. A black cloud dropped over her and she ran to the living room.

"Oh, Meez Candy, the flooring. It is gone," Sancho said.

It had been leaning against the wall right there when she left last night. She looked wildly from one man to another. "Could it be downstairs—or upstairs?"

"It could be, but it ain't," Slade ground out.

Candy still couldn't take it in. "Do you mean it's stolen?"

"Well, I ain't seen no legs on lumber, yet."

Suddenly, she needed the comfort of Chance's strength. "I'm going to call the police," she said tearing out the door. A moment later, she burst into Chance's house—only to find herself looking at a room full of flooring.

She stood, as if nailed down, staring at the lumber. Chance, hearing the door slam, came around the corner. "Hi, how's everything?" He kissed her gently on the cheek.

She still didn't move—or look at him.

"What's wrong, Candy?" No response. He took her shoulders and shook her lightly. "Hey, what's going on?"

She raised her arm and pointed at the lumber. "Wha . . . wha . . . what's my flooring doing here?"

Chance looked at the particleboard, then at her. "Candy, are you joking? That's not your particleboard."

"Don't play games with me, Chance. What are you trying to prove?"

He tried to take her arm but she jerked away.

"Don't you dare touch me." Tears appeared in her eyes. "I really thought you were my friend."

She ran out the door to her car. Throwing herself inside, she laid her head on the steering wheel, sobbing. He was winning. She couldn't fight any longer. But why did he pretend to be so nice? Did he think she was a total airhead?

She sat quietly for some time. Responding to a gentle touch on her hair, she lifted her head and looked into Chance's sad eyes.

"I understand now, Candy. You lost your head for a minute and I'm sure I would have, too." He touched her cheek softly with the back of his fingers.

Unable to control herself, she leaned into his hand.

"Listen, Candy. Please? My particleboard was delivered after you left. I had to help load it into the house. Remember, I couldn't go when you did?"

She stared into his eyes remembering the note, the insulation in his hair, and the bloody bandage on his thumb. Now the flooring. "But you said you had to finish first so you could steal my buyer."

He blanched. "I was kidding. It isn't very funny, is it? Shall I call the police?"

"Yes, please," Candy answered, in a tiny voice.

As the police questioned Candy, all the men from both crews gathered around.

"You have no idea who could have taken the lumber, Miss Hartwell?"

Candy glanced at Chance, then turned her gaze to the floor. "No."

"You're sure it was actually delivered?"

"It came yesterday afternoon. They put it in the living room."

"I don't see any signs of forced entry. What do you think?"

She shrugged, tipping out her hands. "I'm sure I locked up."

"Did any of you guys see anything?" The cop glanced around through the men. They all shrugged or shook their heads.

"Have you considered hiring a security guard, Miss Hartwell?"

"I can't afford it, officer, but my men took turns spending the night all last week. Nothing happened."

The officer rubbed his hand on his pants. "I mean this in all kindness, but as I see it you can't afford not to have someone on duty at all times. Someone is out to get you."

"We will help her, officer police," Sancho offered. "I will stay tonight. I will catch that thief and kill him."

The officer laughed. "Better not go that far." He turned to Candy. "Sorry we weren't more help. I hope you'll think about keeping someone on guard."

"I don't know why you bother with them guys," Slade said. "They don't know nothin'. Well, what we gonna do? Paint the inside?"

"I guess."

Just then, the door opened. "Miss Hartwell?" The young man adjusted the yellow pencil behind his ear. "You want the lumber put where it was yesterday?"

"Yes. How did you know?"

"I dunno, ma'am, I just deliver. What happened to the load

we brought yesterday?"

"Someone stole it." She had an idea. Checking to make sure Chance had gone, she moved closer to the man. "Did you deliver a load just like this to the house next door late yesterday?" she whispered.

"Nope. I get off at four-thirty. You'd have to ask the next shift."

Candy flung her arm down to her side—hard. Another dead end.

The crew flew into the flooring and had the bedroom area and half the living area finished by noon. Like the subflooring, the men cut and placed, and Candy nailed with a gun.

While they ate lunch, the crew divided the remaining nights of the week to watch the place. Even Slade seemed willing this time. Judy and Larry, busy with each other, barely knew what was going on.

That night, Sancho jumped into the car. "Hi, Meez Candy," he said. "I hope the bandito come tonight. He won't bother anybody's house when I quit pounding him."

When they pulled into the lot, Candy caught Sancho's excitement. "You won't be going to bed for a while, will you?"

"I may never go to bed. I catch this guy with bare hands."

"Why don't I leave the car down the street and stay with you for a while?"

He nodded. "Si, I'll take care of you."

They parked a block away, locked the car, and walked to the house. The outside twilight had stolen most of the interior light.

"Let's sit in the entryway where we can watch the door," Candy said. "Can you find something for us to sit on?" He produced two nail kegs.

"I appreciate the loyalty you've shown me," Candy said in the whisper they'd been conversing in.

"Oh, Meez Candy, you're the one who's good. I send almost all my mawnies home and my wife puts it in bank. One of these days I go home and retire. It don't take much mawnies to live down there." He put his hand over his mouth to hide a yawn.

"Shall I leave now so you can—" A small sound at the back door shoved the words back into her throat. Sancho scooted off his keg and crouched behind the stairway, motioning for Candy to get behind him where they were well hidden.

Someone fumbled with the door knob. It opened slowly. A dark form crept inside and closed the door.

Candy held her breath, feeling weak. This was it. They had their man. What were they going to do about it? Sancho's hand shoved her down. She raised back up to watch the man. There he was in the utility room. She could barely see him in the small amount of light flowing through the back window.

He carried something in his hand! She felt Sancho stiffen and realized he had seen it, too. They both ceased breathing as they watched the man stop. What was he doing, anyway?

A moment, later a match flared.

"He's got a fire bomb!" Sancho yelled.

eleven

Sancho dove from his spot behind the stairs, hitting the man with the force of a buffalo stampede. The match went out.

"Hurry, Meez Candy! Get some rope."

"Can I turn on a light now, Sancho?"

"Si. Hurry!"

Candy turned on a light and looked at the two. Sancho's slight frame held the much larger man flat on the floor with no apparent effort.

She found some twine and handed it to Sancho. The man still lay unmoving. "Is he all right?" she asked.

"I dunno, Meez Candy. I hope he's dead. Quick, get your car."

A few minutes later, at the police station, they opened the car doors and jerked out.

Two uniformed policemen met them as they shoved him, still bound tightly, through the heavy doors. "What's going on here?" one of them asked.

Sancho smiled up into their faces. "I bring you a skunk," he said.

The officers looked confused.

"I'm Candy Hartwell," Candy explained. "I hope you know the name."

The policemen looked at each other and shook their heads.

"I'm a builder and that man has been vandalizing my house and stealing materials."

The officers untied the man and brushed him off. As the man teetered on his feet, each officer grabbed an arm. "What do you have to say about this, sir?" the short one asked the man.

The man pulled his arms free, flexed each one, and stretched his legs. Then he bent over several times as though exorcising the pain. "I dunno, offisher. Wha'sh goin' on."

Sancho interrupted, talking fast. "This man take our lumber, break windows, tear up walls, now he try to throw fire bomb in house. We caught him, how you say? Red-handed."

The officer turned to Candy. "Why don't you tell us?" he asked. "Nice and slow."

Candy took a deep breath. "Surely you've heard about the trouble I've been having?"

"Sorry."

"Well, Sancho's right. Someone's been vandalizing my house and stealing my materials, so tonight we stayed in the house to watch. That guy," she nodded at the man who again slouched between the police officers, "came in with a fire bomb in his hand and lit a match. Sancho piled into him in time to save my house." She shrugged. "That's it."

"Were you in this lady's house tonight?" the tall policeman asked the man.

The man tried to focus bleary eyes on Candy. "I don't know."

"You do, too." Candy jumped in front of the man. "Why do you hate me?"

The short gray guy jerked Candy back. "If you don't calm down, lady, I'll have to put you out."

"You'd be upset, too, if he cost you thousands of dollars— dollars you didn't even have." Candy put her hands over her face a moment, then cleared her throat and straightened up "I'm sorry. I'm all right now."

"I think," the other policeman said, "we'd better hold the old man until morning. He isn't in shape to talk now. When we learn anything, we'll call you."

"Okay. Come on, Sancho, I'll take you home. I guess we won't need to watch the place anymore."

When Candy arrived home, she found Judy gone. After two long hours, the younger girl returned excited and happy. "We just went to a movie," she said when Candy questioned her. "I'm not fourteen, you know."

After telling Judy about the man they had caught, Candy fell into bed, said her prayers, especially thanking God for helping them catch the man, and fell asleep before she had time to worry about Judy.

At five o'clock the next morning she drove to the police station.

"What about the guy we caught in my house, officer?" she asked the first blue uniform she saw.

"The old guy? He fell asleep before we could question him anymore. But don't count on him being your man. Looked like an old wino to us."

"What are you talking about? You think there are two guys? We caught that one trying to burn the place down, remember?"

"I remember. Would you like to talk to him?"

"Yes. I have several things I need to know."

She followed the officer down a dimly lit hall to a large cell holding several men. The stale air, reeking of urine, vomit, and alcohol, forced her back. The officer unlocked the door, called the man out, and led them into a room with a small table and several straight chairs.

"You might as well sit down and be comfortable," the officer said, straddling one of the chairs, his arms on the back.

Candy sat down and so did the man.

"All right, sir," the officer said, "state your name and address."

"Name's Wilbur Wright. Ain't got no address."

The officer's face showed no expression. The man seemed more alert this morning, though he reeked of liquor and every breath he expelled nauseated Candy. She moved her chair farther away.

The officer continued his questions. "Why were you in the Hartwell house last night?"

No response.

"Were you in Miss Hartwell's house?"

The filthy, unshaven face peered at Candy. "She Hartwell?"

"Yes, she is."

The man settled back in his chair. "Ain't never seen her before in my life."

The officer jumped to his feet and leaned over the man. "Look here, Wright, she caught you in her house. Why were you there?"

The man sat forward and peered at Candy again. Then he turned to squint at the officer. "I thought I got in a fight somewheres."

"Try to remember what you were doing in her house. I guess that's where you got into the fight."

The man leaned back and rubbed his body in various places. "If I got into a fight with her, I swear I ain't never gonna drink no more."

The officer sat back down. "I think you may as well go," he said. "You can see we aren't on the same wavelength."

"Oh, no! I have a few questions."

The officer settled into a comfortable position and his mouth showed a glimmer of a grin. "Go to it."

Candy stood in front of the man. "Why are you wrecking

my house?" she asked.

He peered up at her through red-rimmed eyes. "Am I wrecking your house?"

"Why do you hate me?"

Wright struggled, trying to think. "Because you beat me up?"

The officer grinned openly now and got up. "Ready to quit?"

"Yes. Let me out of here."

The officer looked down at Wright. "You stay here," he said, "I'll be right back." Then he steered Candy out the way she had come. When they stepped through the outside door, he looked at her quizzically.

Candy gulped in the fresh air. "What's wrong with that man, anyway?"

He shrugged. "Brains are fried from all the junk he drinks. But don't worry. He won't get out of here until he remembers what happened. Then we'll come and check around your place."

Sure. *A lot of checking they would do,* Candy thought, driving to the house. She had seen them check before.

She was the first to arrive at her house but Chance's white van sat in his driveway. She ran over to tell him about the events of the previous night.

"Let's go find the bomb. That'll hang the man," Chance said as they walked across the lots. "I'm sure glad you got him. I don't like you looking at me as though I might be Jack the Ripper."

Candy smiled up at him. "I'm glad, too. I wanted to trust you, though. Really."

"Now, where did Sancho nail him?" Chance asked, looking

down at the floor. He picked up a bottle with a few inches of liquid in the bottom. Shaking it, he twisted off the top and sniffed. "Whew. Cheap wine. Do you know where this stuff came from, Candy?"

A sinking feeling flitted into Candy's stomach so she dropped to her knees and searched the floor. She picked up a broken used match, then a crushed cigarette, and held both articles out to Chance.

He took them and studied the three items a moment, then nodded, "Yep. Here's the firebomb, all right." He put his arm over Candy's shoulder. "Here's the way I figure it. The guy was boozed out of his head and came in to sleep it off. Sancho saw him lighting the cigarette and landed on him with fourteen tons of fury."

Candy nodded mutely.

Chance grinned. "Shall we chuck the evidence?"

She shook her head. "My Heavenly Father wouldn't like that. Also, now that you've wrecked our theory, you're suspect again. I'm kidding. But seriously, if that's not the guy, then the other one will be back."

"He sure will. And it's not me." He pulled her to him for a quick hug.

A moment later, Hugh Perry, the police officer, strode through the door. "I hear you had some excitement here last night. I'd like to check it out if you don't mind."

"Too late, Officer Perry," Candy said. "We already did."

Chance handed the wine to the officer, then the crushed cigarette and broken match.

"What's this?"

"It's the fire bomb, Hugh."

The officer looked at the objects some more, then back to Chance. Chance took the wine bottle, unscrewed the top, and poked it under the officer's nose. "It's this way. You drink the wine, swallow it, then light the cigarette, and voila! You blow up the place."

Candy gave Chance a shove. "He's giving me a bad time because in the dark, I thought these things were a fire bomb."

A light turned on in Hugh Perry's eyes. "You mean there's no bomb?"

"Afraid not." Candy leaned against the wall. "I guess the guy gets turned loose, huh?"

"Yeah. And if you didn't have any enemies before, you do now."

"I guess." Candy remembered back to the night before. "We really roughed him up."

The policeman looked up and down Candy's frail five-foot frame. "I don't think you hurt him much."

Candy laughed. "I'm only a woman, is that it? Well, last night I packed a punch."

The other men arrived and Sancho hurried to Candy. "Did the man confess his crimes, Meez Candy?"

Candy picked up the wine bottle and showed it to Sancho. "Does this look familiar?"

Sancho shook his black head.

"Sancho, look at these things." She showed him the match and cigarette.

He shook his head again. "Is not mine."

She laughed and roughed his hair. "Sancho, these things are our fire bomb."

He took each item and examined it. "You mean that man wasn't him?"

"That's right. You got the wrong man," Officer Perry said.

Sancho sat down on the stairs and wrapped his brown arms around his head. "Ooh, we hurt him, no?"

Chance sat down beside the little man. "Look," he said, "you may still have saved the house. If he'd gone to sleep with a lighted cigarette he could have burned the house down accidentally."

At lunch, Chance asked Candy to stay after everyone else left.

"Okay, you have five minutes," she checked her watch, "until twelve-fifty-eight." She laughed and looked into his eyes that radiated love.

"Okay," he said, "I don't quite know how to say this."

"Say it."

"Okay, I will. I'm wondering how you're planning to finance the completion of your house, since you seem to insist on doing everything twice."

"I'm trying to figure that out."

"Why don't you let me help you?"

"Wow! That's the nicest thing anyone's said to me all day. Let me think about your offer, okay? And thanks."

Candy was half across her lot when she had to ask Chance a question. "Hey, how did you know I was in trouble?" she called.

"A little bird," he yelled back.

"Uh-huh. A Judy Bird?"

He didn't answer, but raised his hand in a big wave and stepped inside.

When Candy went inside, the men had the paint rollers, trays, and handles out and were mixing the paint. They would have the first coat on by noon tomorrow.

At five o'clock Candy took all the rollers, brushes, and pans to the water faucet to wash. She hated the job so intensely that she never asked anyone to help. Leaning over the faucet, she let the water run through the roller, on and on and on.

As she ran the millionth gallon of water through the rollers she heard a siren. Well, she would rather be washing rollers than be the poor people in the wreck. The siren grew louder. The emergency vehicle turned down their street. She stood up to watch it go past, but it didn't. It turned into Chance's driveway.

Someone was hurt over there! She took off for the house next door.

Running through the house and out the back door, she found paramedics kneeling beside a man on the ground. Chance's crew crowded behind the paramedics. No one said a word. She pushed her way to where she could see. Chance! He lay quietly with his eyes closed—and blood ran everywhere.

twelve

Candy cupped her hand over her mouth to keep from crying out as the paramedics cut Chance's pant leg off almost to the top, just below a tourniquet they had applied. A gaping wound, eight inches long and wide open, at least four inches across, claimed Candy's gaze. Though blood saturated his clothes, it only oozed from the wound. Whitish fat glistened in the opening.

They worked on him a few more minutes. Then they lifted his huge body onto the gurney then into the van. A moment later, the unit pulled away. Lights flashing, the siren remained silent.

Candy collapsed to the ground and took several deep breaths.

"He's going to be okay," Judy said.

Candy took several more long breaths.

Judy sat down and hugged her. "Do you really care that much, Can? I thought you couldn't stand the guy."

Candy met Judy's eyes and smiled. "I care."

Judy got up, took Candy's hand, and pulled her up, too. "Come on, let's go home. We'll get your car later."

Candy looked around and found every man from Chance's crew watching her. Every face showed the shock of the accident. "Will you be all right, Miss Hartwell?" Johnny asked.

"She's fine," Judy said. "I'll take care of my sister." Candy followed Judy to her car, glad to lean on her big little sister.

The half-washed paint rollers dried in the sun.

At home, Judy shoved Candy into the bathroom and went

to make supper. *Chance had to be all right*, Candy thought as she showered, or they would have had the sirens going when they left, rather than just the lights. *Thank You, Lord. Oh thank You, bless You and praise Your Holy Name!*

She ate a plate of Judy's hastily prepared supper and drank a glass of milk. "Thanks, Judy. That was nice. Now—"

"I know, you want to go to the hospital. Just give me a minute to wash off the day's sweat and stink."

Inside the hospital, Candy approached the information desk. "I'd like Jeremy Chancellor's room number, please."

"Room 212. Oh, I see he isn't allowed visitors, yet."

"Thank you," Candy said, taking off down the hall.

Halfway down the hall, Judy reached for Candy's shoulder. "Where you going, Can?"

"Room 212."

After wandering the halls, the girls found the room. Judy went to a nearby waiting room and Candy, after looking both ways, hurried inside.

Chance lay flat with clear fluid dripping into one arm and something that looked like blood going into the other. Sleeping quietly, or possibly even unconscious, he looked totally vulnerable.

"You're going to get well quick," she whispered. "I know you are because God wants us together." She looked at him again, taking in his terribly pale face. "Oh, Chance, you have to. I love you so much," she added still in a whisper.

His eyes still closed, Chance grinned and crooked his finger for her to come closer.

She backed two steps away.

"Come here, Candy," he said, opening his eyes. "Come over here where you can hear me."

Had he heard her say she loved him?

"What happened to your leg?" she asked, changing the subject.

"Someone knocked me onto a saw. No big deal."

"What did they do to you?"

"Forty-four stitches and a lot of blood, I guess."

"You don't look so good."

He grinned. "I'm sure I've felt better at some time in my life, but never happier. I expect to get out of here tomorrow. How are we celebrating our engagement?"

"We aren't engaged."

"But you said . . . ."

"Forget what I said. I always get light-headed when someone gets hurt. I was there before they hauled you away, and saw a lot of blood."

Chance looked disappointed. "Okay, I guess I am pretty tired, but couldn't we celebrate my coming home from the hospital?"

"Sure. We'll think of something." She kissed him on the forehead and tiptoed back to Judy.

They hadn't been home a half hour when Larry came along and honked for Judy. "I'll be back pretty soon," she told Candy. "We're going after your car." Judy did bring Candy's car home—at one-thirty in the morning.

"Where have you been?" Candy asked, doing her best to remain calm.

Judy grinned. "Around. Aren't you going to thank me?"

"You're never going with him again, understand?"

"Look, Can," Judy said patiently, "I'm going with him anytime I want so you may as well get used to it." And then she continued:

"When I was a little girl, you told me what to do.

Those days are gone now, because I'm big like you.
I get up and go to work each day, and stay until I'm
through.

So let me choose my own path. My brain is grownup,
too."

Candy felt crushed at Judy's message and fell into bed
crying to God. As she lay exhausted, a Bible verse came to her
mind as though someone were reading it to her. *Do not be
anxious about anything, but in everything, by prayer and
petition, with thanksgiving, present your requests to God. And
the peace of God, which transcends all understanding, will
guard your hearts and your minds in Christ* Jesus. (Phil. 4:6-
7) "Thank you, Lord," she whispered. "Please, please give me
this peace. Help me to help Judy all I can—and accept what
I can't change." She fell asleep feeling closer to Him than she
had for a while.

The next day when the workers descended on the picnic
tables, Chance hobbled over on crutches looking extremely
pale. When he reached the table, two of his workers took his
arms and helped him sit down.

"You idiotic fool!" Candy said, delighted to see him. "You
truly think you're indispensable, don't you?"

Chance opened his big lunch box, pulled out a sandwich,
and unwrapped it. "Well, I mostly came to see you." He
shoved half a sandwich into his mouth.

As Candy considered Chance's statement, she saw a famil-
iar-looking figure approaching the table. As the dirty stum-
bling man got within smelling distance, she remembered
him—the bum from a few nights ago.

"Hello, Miss Hartwell. Still working on your house, I see,"

he said.

"Yes, Mr. Wright, we keep on. What are you up to?"

The man sat down beside Candy, swinging his legs over the bench and under the table. "Oh, just passing by and your food smelled good."

Candy moved away from Wright until her shoulder touched Sancho's, scooting her lunch along with her. "Oh," she said, not looking at Wright, "would you like one of my sandwiches?" She shoved it in front of him, together with a paper napkin.

He ate the sandwich, saying nothing. The table quieted until the only sounds were paper rustling and food crunching.

When Wilbur Wright finished his sandwich he wiped his lips elaborately with the napkin. "That was right good. Too bad I'm still hungry."

Chance tossed a couple of cookies onto the bare table in front of the filthy man. An apple, a banana, chips, and several more cookies followed Chance's offering.

Wright ate everything that came his way. "Good food sure makes a fella thirsty, doesn't it?" he asked when he finished.

"See that hose over there?" Chance growled. "Turn it on and drink all you want."

Wright disentangled himself from the table, strolled to the hose and took a sip of water. Then he returned and grinned down at Candy. "D'ja ever find the guy you thought I was?"

She didn't look at him. "Not yet."

"Well, ain't you sorry you beat me up?"

Candy met his eyes. "Yes, I'm sorry, but you shouldn't have been trespassing."

He looked around at the listening men. "I hope she don't never get mad at you guys."

Chance wiped his forehead. "She's always mad at me."

"Does she beat you black-and-blue?"

"Not quite."

"Well, you should've seen her get me. I'm thinking of suing her for a bundle . . . if you know what I mean."

"No," Chance said, "I don't know what you mean. Why don't you tell us."

Sancho hopped up from the table. "But Meez Candy, don't he know?"

"Shut up, Sancho, and get to work," Candy snapped.

Sancho walked off, shaking his head. The other workers gathered up their things and disappeared into the two houses, leaving Chance and Candy with Wright.

"Come on, Wright, what were you saying?" Chance ground out.

"I was bruised from my head to my feet, and so sore I could hardly move. I still hurt when I walk or bend over. I think the little lady owes me for allowing her to use me for a punching bag. A thousand bucks should be about right."

Candy's mouth dropped open.

"Not a chance," Chance said. "She should sue you for trespassing."

Wright grinned and rubbed the back of his head. "She already got me. Now it's my turn to get her."

"Well, you're crazy if you think I'm giving you a thousand dollars," Candy snapped. "So sue."

Wright tipped his battered felt hat. "I'll feel guilty suing a tiny little woman, but if that's the way it is."

Chance, still seated at the table, held a bill toward Wright. "Here, this is all you get so don't show your face around here again."

Wright lurched over and snatched the money, looked at both sides, then took off down the street holding the bill against his chest, grinning as though he had won the lottery.

Candy watched him a moment, then sat down beside Chance. "Whew. That had to be some kind of comedown. How much did you give him?"

"Ten bucks. He just needed some wine." Chance looked back toward his house then at Candy and grinned. "Now, how am I supposed to get back to the house?"

She got up. "Tell me what to do."

"Well, could you lean the crutches against the table, then help me get my legs over the bench? I don't handle these things very well yet."

Candy scrambled to do as he asked and, in a few minutes, they inched toward his house, Chance looking very pale and unsteady on his feet.

"Does it hurt a lot?" she asked.

"Hardly at all," he said, wincing with every step. "In a couple of days I'll be as good as new. I guess we'll celebrate then, okay?"

"Sure. Unless you'd like to come to my house today and rest on the couch while I make dinner."

"I'd like that. Maybe I'll leave my car here and ride with you."

"Great. Now, you take it easy this afternoon."

Late in the afternoon, Candy went to the car after some nails. As she was searching through the tiny trunk, someone drove up to Chance's house. He looked familiar so Candy watched him go in.

The man's name popped into her head. Pete Meyer! The man Dad had fired. The man who had asked her for a job a couple of times and had gotten nasty when she declined. She felt very uncomfortable with him around. She returned to finish the dining room floor, the last to be nailed down.

Returning to her car an hour later, Candy found Chance in the back seat with his bad leg lying on the seat. "Ready to go?"

"Ready. Your car sure is little."

"Sorry," she started the car and backed into the street. "What did Pete Meyer want?"

"You really do keep track of what goes on at my house, don't you? The guy wanted a job, but I told him I'm having trouble keeping my regular help busy."

"Was he nice?"

"No. He told me what he thought of me—and added some choice words for you. What did you do to him?"

"Not me. Dad fired him. And I wouldn't rehire him."

"Well, not to worry. To quote the man, he's leaving this biased, prejudiced, one-horse town that refuses to give a man a second chance."

Candy felt relieved that the nasty man would be gone and she could forget him.

When they arrived home, she settled Chance on the couch and joined Judy in the kitchen to help with supper.

"Is he spending the night?" Judy asked as she scraped two carrots for the salad.

"I hadn't thought about it."

After supper, they started a game of Scrabble, putting the board on the coffee table beside the couch so Chance could easily reach it, but he dropped off to sleep between each turn.

After a while, Judy signaled Candy to come to the kitchen. "It's not like him to fall asleep all the time," she whispered. "He'd better spend the night."

"Hey, where'd everyone go?" Chance called.

Judy went in. "We had a little conference and decided you should stay here for a couple of days."

A look of relief passed over Chance's face, then worry.

"That would be great, Judy, except I have some things to do. Candy, could you take me back to my rig? Thanks for the invite anyway."

Judy drove Chance's beat-up white van home while Candy drove Chance. Candy ordered Chance to stay away from work one more day.

The next morning, Candy left early so she could rent a paint sprayer and pick up paint for the outside.

"Miss Hartwell, you're going to have to get a larger rig," the paint salesman said smiling, after cramming the equipment into her small car. "Now, what color did you choose for the paint?"

Candy opened her purse, then remembered she had left the paint chip on the bottom step of the spiral stairway. "I'll be back in a little while," she said.

She drove to the house wondering if she were getting senile. Well, to avoid losing more time, the guys could be getting the sprayer hooked up to the electricity and whatever else they needed to do which she went back for the paint.

She jumped from the car while it was still rolling and she ran into the house. Before she reached the stairs, she saw the red words screaming at her from the white entryway walls WOMAN GO HOME! TRY, TRY, YOU STILL AIN'T A MAN! The writing had been spray-painted onto her newly finished walls.

Feeling sick to her stomach, she ran up the stairs into the kitchen. WOMAN YORE MAKIN A FOOL OF YERSELF appeared on each kitchen wall.

Running to the dining room she read on all three walls: WOMEN AIN'T GOT WHAT MEN HAS SO WHY TRY? She ran through the house. The vandal hadn't missed a single wall, let alone a room. Sitting on the stairs, she noticed the paint chip and shoved it into her pocket.

Buck came in the back door and, seeing Candy sitting on the stairs, stopped. "Did you notice the back door glass is broken again?" he asked.

Candy sighed. "No, but I noticed the rest of the house. Take a look."

A moment later Slade, Luke, and Sancho joined the trek through the house. The master bedroom seemed to have the gem on its walls. BEAT YOUR BRAINS OUT WOMAN. YOU STILL AIN'T SMART ENOUGH TO BE A MAN.

Candy struggled into the master bath and dropped to the floor. "Father," she cried, tears running down her cheeks, "You promised You wouldn't let any more happen than we can bear." She sobbed another moment and raised her eyes. "This is more than I can bear," she whispered toward the ceiling. After a while she felt some peace and decided she could bear this one more thing. "I guess we'll repaint the inside today," she told her men.

"Can't paint over that stuff," Slade said.

Candy looked at him in horror. "What do you mean, can't? We have to."

thirteen

Everyone cooperated, and new white paint soon glistened on the walls in the three upstairs bedrooms. But, when Candy stepped back to check, she saw every word coming through the paint.

"Slade!" she bellowed.

"What now?" he answered, rushing into the room.

She pointed at the wall. "Look."

"I told you—"

"What do we do now?" she interrupted.

"Sand the walls down and start over. That means the drywall people will have to come back, too."

"Where's the money coming from?"

"Well, the sooner we get started, the sooner we finish," Slade said. "Why don't I take Luke and do the outside as we planned? The rest of you can sand walls."

"I have a better idea," Candy said. "Why don't we all do the outside? By tomorrow I may be able to face this mess." In a little while the outside of the house began to take on a rich dark natural color.

When they shut down for lunch, Candy's crew eagerly told Chance about the new splurge of vandalism.

Chance listened patiently until he had an opening. "You don't need to sand and retexture," he said quietly.

Slade's ears pricked up. "Yeah, hotshot? You didn't see that stuff bleed right through the paint. How you gonna stop that?"

"Easy." He turned to Candy, his bleary eyes eager. "Just enamel the whole house, then if you want flat paint, paint over it. I've noticed lots of builders are using enamel for the whole house anyway You might think about that. It's a more durable and eloquent-looking finish."

Slade jeered. "I suppose you learned that trick in college?"

Chance laughed. "As a matter of fact, I didn't. One of the guys stomped a lid onto a can of wood stain. When we looked up, the wall had black splotches from the ceiling to the floor. We tried all the hard things before we experimented with enamel. Believe me, it covers."

"Thanks," Candy said. "I'll try it this afternoon. Now I know why you came to work today against my orders. Are you taking it easy?"

Chance grinned. "Yeah. Johnny brought a lawn chair."

Slade looked sharply at Chance. "Looks to me like you're gettin' around plenty good."

"Better."

"Where were you last night?"

Chance looked surprised, then glanced at Candy. "Around, why?"

"Just wondered," Slade grunted. "Don't take much strength to use spray paint. Shore seems strange to me, every time we start gittin' ahead somethin' happens to our house."

"Seems strange to me, too," Chance said, climbing gingerly away from the table and hobbling to his house.

"Chance wouldn't sabotage us," Candy said.

Slade cocked his head toward Chance's house. "He shore took off in a hurry."

That afternoon, Candy and Sancho enameled the bedroom area while the others used the sprayer on the outside.

"How does it look?" she asked as they finished the last room.

Sancho grinned from ear to ear. "Just fine, Meez Candy. I

don't see nothing but white."

"Me, too. The red paint's covered," she agreed, happily. "You can go now, Sancho. We'll do the rest of the house tomorrow. Right now, I'm going to tell Chance."

After she told Chance, he grabbed her hand and her pulled her down to him. "My pay for the tip," he said, kissing her softly on the lips.

She dropped to her knees beside his chair and kissed him again. His lips tasted sweet and soft. She kissed him again. "Your reward for the tip," she whispered against his lips.

A moment later, she ran from the house and jumped into her car. What was Chance doing to her? She couldn't think clearly anymore.

As she drove onto the street, she thought about Slade's remarks. Progress on Chance's house was slow at the moment all right. No doubt about that. But Chance hurt her? Never. She hoped.

That night, Candy expressed her continuing doubts to Judy, who went into orbit. "Can!" she yelled. "You used to ask *me* what Jesus would do. Well, do you think He'd keep accusing someone after His Father had showed Him the person was innocent?"

Candy admitted He wouldn't and asked Him to give her a large dose of faith.

A little later, Judy came from her room. "Candy, listen to this," she said.

"God spoke to you. Were you listening?
Are you remembering?
You heard with joy, then doubt crept in.
Faith fled.
He never makes mistakes, you know.

When He says it you can count on it
FOREVER."

Candy jumped up and hugged her wise big little sister. "That was beautiful, Judy. Maybe I can learn from you, now that you're all grown up."

Meanwhile, Candy kept wondering what she could do about the vandalism. Whoever was doing it kept right at it. Maybe her men should watch the house every night until it was finished. Someone really had it in for her—or all women. But Candy thought it was personal.

Once more, the guys volunteered to watch the house and did so for the next five days with nothing happening. Although Candy desperately wanted them to continue watching, she didn't beg them. After all, she couldn't pay them. If she could pay she would never leave her house unguarded one night until she had it finished and sold.

One day, she and Luke put up wallpaper in the kitchen, living room, entryway, and master bedroom. The place would be ready for sale in two weeks—if there was no more vandalism.

"Anyone home?" Chance called from the doorway, interrupting Candy's thoughts. He walked in and looked at the paper. "Looks great. Want to do mine next?"

As he walked in, the room seemed to brighten a few shades. He walked without the aid of crutches now, but was still stiff-legged.

"Your house looks as nice as mine and you know it," she said, her eyes shining.

"How do you like the way I'm getting around?" he asked. The left corner of his lip twitched. "Don't you think I'm about as good as new?"

"Strange you should mention it. I was just thinking how well you're doing. I'm proud of you."

"Glad to hear you say it. When do we go out to celebrate?"

"I've forgotten what we're celebrating," Candy admitted, "but you name it."

"Tonight."

"Name the time. I'll be ready a half hour early."

"How about six o'clock? We'll make it an evening."

"I'll be ready."

"I'm glad you're going, Can," Judy said when Candy told her about her date. "I worry about you when I have all the fun."

When the doorbell rang, Candy rushed to a mirror for a last check. Her dark hair curled softly all over, falling gently over her shoulders. She nodded. It had turned out okay.

She had chosen a barely used, cranberry silk dress with wide ruffles that she wore slightly off her shoulders. Cranberry lipstick matched her dress perfectly and a touch of eye shadow and blush gave her an elegantly dainty look. Exactly the effect she wanted.

When she opened the door, Chance stepped back and stared. Then he stared some more. He rubbed his chin thoughtfully. "Are you the lady builder working on the lot next to mine?" he asked quietly. "Or are you a vision I dreamed up?"

Candy laughed appreciatively. "Let's go. I'm hungry."

After helping her into the car, he limped around the front. His black dinner jacket and tie with his white shirt made his blond hair look even lighter and his tan darker. He seemed so straight and honest. And if he didn't truly care for her, he was such a fantastic actor that he should be making big bucks in front of a television camera. No, he shouldn't. He really did care for her. She knew he did. The look she kept seeing in his eyes was no act. She felt as if her own eyes must mirror the look—and that wasn't an act either.

But who could be mean enough to keep vandalizing my house? she wondered.

"Are you still hungry?" he asked, as he settled into his own seat and started the engine.

"Of course I'm hungry. I'm the lady builder from next door."

"Tonight I'm taking you to a place worthy of a beautiful woman."

"Thanks." No man had ever made her feel so special. Her breath came in quick gulps and her mouth felt as if it were full of cotton. She wanted so badly to let go and just revel in their love. But she couldn't relax until she knew who was hurting her—even though she knew it wasn't Chance.

"Shall we go in? Or do you plan to sit here and dream the night away?" Chance said quietly, standing outside her open door. He waved a big paw in front of her eyes.

Coming to with a start, she jumped out, and, slipping her arm through Chance's, proudly walked inside with the most handsome man in the place.

"Well," he said, settling her back in the car two hours later, "you looked and acted like a dream that came to life, but you ate like a builder." He grinned through half-closed eyes.

"The food was wonderful and the ambiance delightful. I've never been in such a fancy place. Thanks again."

Chance stopped at a red light and turned to Candy. "It's been wonderful. But the night's still young. Let's not quit yet."

"Okay. What would you like to do?"

As the light turned green, Chance pulled across the intersection and to the curb. Turning off the motor, he pulled Candy close to him.

She turned her face up for the whisper of a kiss he offered. Then he buried his face in her hair. "Oh, Candy, you don't know what you do to me." He patted her hair then fluffed it around her face and carefully arranged it on her shoulders. "You're so beautiful you drive me mad. You care for me, too. At least a little?"

Candy sighed. "I care. Oh Chance, I care so much. But I'm so mixed up right now my mind is a shambles."

Chance sighed and fiddled with the key, finally putting it into the ignition. "Is it someone else?"

Candy turned to face him in the illumination from the street lights. "No! It's you."

He pulled out the key and dangled it between his fingers. "Okay, let's have it. Is there something about me that turns you off? Bad breath? The way I dress? I know I need a haircut. Go ahead, I can handle it. I might even be able to change it."

Candy swallowed. She swallowed again, but the lump remained. Should she tell him? "It's the vandalism, Chance. I don't know who's my friend anymore—or my enemy."

His face tensed. "Come on, Candy, you can do better than that." He dangled the keys from his index finger. "The car isn't moving until you tell me what's wrong."

She drew in a long breath. "Well, I tried to think it was Pete Meyer, but he's out of the country now . . . and there's been too much to be him. It's just that . . . uh . . . you cut your thumb when my windows got broken, you had insulation in your hair when my wiring and insulation got ripped out, and you're the . . . uh . . . only person who'd have anything to gain if I gave up."

He sat up sharply and grasped the steering wheel. "I'm— WHAT!" He sat stiffly a moment then sighed, shoved the key into the ignition, and roared into the traffic.

On the way home, neither spoke a word. He drove into her driveway, braked sharply, and piled out. When he slammed his door closed, Candy could tell he was very upset.

Limping around the car, he jerked her door open and started

up the sidewalk to the house without looking back to see if she followed. "It's been nice," he said when they reached the front door. "I'll probably see you tomorrow." The tone of his voice said it hadn't been all that nice and he would rather not see her tomorrow—or ever, if that could be possible. He limped back to the car, slammed the door again, and roared away.

Candy stood on the porch for a moment gathering her wits, then unlocked the door and went inside.

"Hi, Can, how'd it go?" Judy called from the living room.

Stepping in, Candy found Judy sitting under a lamp, writing a letter.

"Not well, Judy. Not well at all."

"Come on, Can. I peeked through the door when he came for you. I never saw anyone so gorgeous in my whole life. What's not to go well?"

Candy sighed and sat down. "Well, would you believe I told him I suspect him of my vandalism?"

Judy wrote a couple of lines, then laid her pen and pad on the coffee table. She gave Candy her full attention. "Not again! You couldn't have done it again. Tell me you didn't."

"Afraid I did."

"Can, you're a fool," Judy said "If you knew Chance you'd know he'd never hurt anyone. You'd also know he thinks you're extra special. And in the second place, if you had a grain of faith, you'd remember that God's told you a million times that Chance isn't doing it. Remember, Can, when God says something, it's true and it's forever. I think this whole thing's to teach you some faith."

Candy couldn't disagree with that and fell asleep praying for faith so the lesson could be over.

The next morning, as she drove to work, she started thinking again. No question about it, Chance's and her houses were so similar that the same buyer would be looking at both. If he finished first, some strong competition would be eliminated. If she completely gave up, he would have a clear field in the whole subdivision. "Candy," she scolded out loud, "it's been less than a day since you got all your new faith. Will you never learn?"

When she opened the front door to her new house, she smelled wood finisher. The guys must be nearly through with the cabinets.

She quietly closed the door and headed for Chance's house to clear the air.

When she got there, he was standing on a ladder beside one of his windows, hanging a shutter. "Hi, what are you doing on that ladder?" she asked lightly.

"Somebody has to do it," he said between clenched teeth.

"Your house is really pretty, Chance. No doubt about it, you have class."

He responded with an unintelligible grunt.

Candy swallowed. "Chance, could we talk?"

"Go ahead."

"Please? I mean really talk. I can't talk to your back while you work. Could we go to the picnic tables?"

He put another screw in the shutter.

"Chance," she finally said, "I'm going to go sit at the table until you come. I hope it's before the herd comes at noon. Please." Candy walked to the tables and sat on the side her crew always did.

He glanced over his shoulder at her and laboriously climbed the few steps to the ground, limped to his front porch, and leaned the next shutter against the house. Then he limped over. Lifting his leg over the bench, he deposited it under the table and faced Candy, folding his hands in front of him on the table. He still didn't say a word.

"I'm sorry, Chance. I wouldn't hurt you for all the world but my brain's so scrambled I can't think straight."

He studied his hands.

She reached across the table and covered his hands with hers. "Please, will you help me?"

His eyes snapped to meet hers, surprise clearly shining through the deep blue. "How could I help you?"

"Help me think straight. Tell me what to do."

He pulled his arms back and folded his hands in his lap under the table. "I can't tell you what to do. You're your own woman with your own ideas, as you keep reminding me."

Candy folded her hands on the table. "I know you aren't doing it, Chance, but I'm desperate. I've already used all the money in my building loan and owe thousands of dollars that aren't covered. The suppliers expect to be paid within thirty days. When that time's gone, I'm in big trouble. I have to find out who it is and stop him."

"Good luck."

"Come on, don't be mean. What would you do if it were your house?"

Chance gave the question some thought. "I suppose I'd sleep in the house every night until it sold. But you can't do that, since you're just a woman."

Candy thought she saw his lip twitch just a tiny bit, and maybe his eyes sparkled ever so slightly, but his face remained stony cold.

"Who says I can't? I have to defend my property, don't I?"

His eyes flashed. "I say you can't. The stuff that's been happening to your house isn't child's play. He'd make short work of a scrawny little wimp like you."

fourteen

Candy took a few seconds to absorb Chance's strong words. He definitely didn't want her to stay at the house. That could be because he didn't want her hurt. Or could it be that he didn't want her to discover him? "So what am I supposed to do?" she finally asked. "You and everyone else in the world knows I don't have the money to hire a guard."

Chance sighed with exaggerated patience. "Like the cop said a long time ago, maybe you can't afford not to."

"Chance," Candy said quietly as though talking to a small child, "I don't have any money at all. How does a person hire a guard when she doesn't have money to pay the guy? You don't realize what a mess I'm in. If I luck out, I may be able to stretch my credit to sixty days. I have no idea what I'm going to do after that. I'm living on hope and prayer for an early buyer. If one doesn't happen along, I'm dead. Maybe I should take out bankruptcy right now before I run up a lot more bills. Is that what I should do, Chance? I don't know what to do or where to go anymore."

"Let me lend you the money. Maybe that would prove me innocent."

Chance covered her small hand with his greater one and this time she pulled back. "I don't want you to prove your innocence. We both know you'd never be involved in something like this. I appreciate your offer of help, and I may end up accepting it. I'm almost against the wall."

Chance lifted his leg over the bench. "I better get back to work."

125

"Don't go, Chance. Please, not quite yet."

Settling back on the bench with his back to the table and Candy, he sighed. "I don't know what more we have to say. I'm sorry I'm not in condition right now to tangle with this jerk myself or I'd volunteer my services."

She sat and watched him get up and limp heavily to his house.

The next day, she and her men installed the cabinets in the kitchen and one bathroom before the two crews gathered for lunch. While they ate, a large delivery truck drove up to Candy's house and she jumped up to meet the driver.

She came back laughing. "The stove top, oven, dishwasher, microwave, and trash compactor are here. I can't believe my house is so nearly finished."

For the first time since they had started eating, Chance met her eyes. "Congratulations, Candy. You're going to beat me by several days."

Sancho leaned over the table so he could see Candy from the other end. "Meez Candy," he called, "you think someone should watch appliances?"

"Ugh!" Candy hadn't thought of the possibility of their being stolen. "I think so, Sancho. Maybe I'll stay."

"Oh, no, you won't," Chance bellowed.

"I'll stay," Luke volunteered.

"Okay, thanks." Candy tossed him a grateful smile.

"It's going to be several days before you get them nailed down, isn't it?" Chance asked.

"Afraid so."

"I'll watch tomorrow, Meez Candy. I watch good."

"Sure," Slade snarled. "We know how you watch. The rest of you guys just be sure you don't show up that night or you'll be killed."

"You guys ain't talking about getting a guard, are you?" Wilbur Wright asked, coming around the corner of the house.

"Oh, hello, Willie," Chance said. "Just passing through, I hope.

"Yeah, I guess. Just going by and smelled lunches." He sat on the end of the bench by Candy.

She took one whiff, lost her appetite, and handed him her halfeaten sandwich.

He grabbed it with two hands and shoved most of it into his mouth.

"Look here," Chance said, "these people need their lunches. They work hard but I guess you don't know what that is."

Wright shoved the rest of the sandwich in, and chewed thoughtfully. "Well, ain't that sumpin'? I just came here looking for a job. I heard someone's tearing up your building. I could guard it when ain't no one else around. Bein's I'm a night person, I'd be a natural for—"

Hoots of laughter interrupted the malodorous man.

"Yeah," Buck said, after things quieted, "you're such a night person you don't even know who clobbered you the other day."

Wright glanced at Candy quizzically. "I don't? The cops said the tough lady builder did it. I'm barely over the soreness."

Candy gave Buck a quick look to shut him up.

He shrugged. "If you're such a night person, why did the cops have to tell you who beat you up?"

Candy shook her head. "I'm sorry, Mr. Wright. I wish I could hire a guard, but I can't." She thrust the remainder of her lunch toward the ragged-looking man. "At least I'm not hungry, so go ahead and finish my lunch."

Wright didn't have to be asked twice.

The next day, Candy and her crew finished installing cabinets. The vinyls were in and Candy ran from room to room admiring the house.

"I don't blame you a bit. It looks beautiful."

Candy spun around to find Chance watching her with an amused smile. "When will you have the appliances installed?" he asked thoughtfully.

"Tomorrow, I think. They're going to be our first priority, now that we have the cabinets in."

"Good." He turned and hobbled out of the house.

That evening, as Candy drove out after Sancho, she felt security in the knowledge that he would be watching the appliances for her. Hopefully, they would be installed tomorrow.

As she turned in to the old trailer, she noticed it looked different. Fresh paint gave it a clean look and the ripped-out spot in the side seemed to be gone.

Sancho climbed in, interrupting her inspection. "Thank you, Meez Candy. I will keep your things safe for you tonight."

"I'm thanking you, Sancho. I really appreciate your good help. Say, the trailer looks different. Did you do something to it?"

"*Si*, sure. I paint outside and inside. I fix big hole, too."

"Why did you go to so much trouble? It isn't even yours."

"I use house, I fix house."

Candy cast him a look of admiration and started the car.

Candy returned home just in time to see Judy running to Larry's pickup. After she climbed in, he drove away.

When Judy returned at eleven-thirty, Candy pretended to be asleep. It wouldn't do any good to yell, and she didn't feel like acting as if she didn't care. She did care. If she could stop that friendship she would do it no matter what.

Early the next morning, she made breakfast and packed a lunch for Sancho as well as for herself and Judy. He might be small, Candy thought, but he eats like a builder.

When she arrived at her house, she noticed Chance's white van already parked in his driveway. "Hi, Sancho," she called, unlocking the front door. The house creaked in reply.

Striding through the entryway, she opened the utility room door.

Sancho lay on the bare floor, several feet from the cot. She ran and knelt beside him. "Sancho, what are you doing?"

He stirred and moaned, then put his hand to his head. A moment later, he opened his eyes wide and stared at Candy.

"What's the matter?" asked Candy.

"Ooh, my head." He rubbed the back of it.

Suddenly Candy felt frightened. "Are you all right, Sancho? What's wrong with your head?"

"You feel, Meez Candy?"

He steered her hand to a huge lump on his head. Then she noticed blood in his hair and on the floor.

"Sancho, what happened?"

"You better check appliances. I think he hit me with something."

Candy rushed up the stairs into the living room where the appliances had been stacked. The bare room looked huge! Not one of the several large cardboard boxes remained. Candy sank to the floor in shock. Those appliances had cost thousands of dollars.

Then, she remembered Sancho. Running back to the utility room, she found him sitting on his cot with his head in his hands, drops of blood oozing through his fingers.

"Don't move," she said, "I'm going over to Chance's place to call an ambulance."

He looked up. "No, no, Meez Candy, I'm all right. I just rest a little."

"You have to be checked, Sancho, but don't worry, we have insurance to cover it. Would you rather go in my car?"

He hung his head. "I never been to doctor. I don't know how."

She laughed and took his hand. "You don't have to know how. The doctor knows how. Are you able to walk to the car?"

He stood up, wobbled a bit, and sat back down.

"It's all right," she assured him, "I'll get Chance to help put you in the car."

As she bolted through the door, she almost ran into Slade. "Come help me put Sancho in my car, quick!"

Slade raised an eyebrow. "I reckon if that Mexican don't want to go in your car it ain't no business of mine."

Candy grabbed his arm. "Come on. Sancho's been hurt."

Slade ambled into the utility room and stood looking down at the now trembling man. "Too much to drink, Gomez?"

"Slade! Help me put him into my car." Candy felt tears behind her eyes but was determined to keep them there until she had taken care of Sancho. "Come on, Slade, I can't do it alone."

They each put an arm around the little man and easily put him into the car. Fearing the way Sancho trembled, she broke the speed limit getting to the hospital.

As she rested in the waiting room, a policeman approached her. "Miss Hartwell?"

She stood up. "Yes, I'm Candy Hartwell."

The officer pointed to the seat Candy had vacated. "Please, sit down."

Candy sat.

"I need to ask you a few questions," he said, taking the adjoining chair. "Do you know what happened to Mr. Gomez?

I understand you're his employer." He pulled out a pad and short pencil, giving the pencil lead a sound lick with his tongue.

"Yes, I know what happened. He was guarding my place and someone knocked him over the head and stole my appliances. If you'd caught the man earlier, this wouldn't have happened."

The suppressed tears decided to dump all over and Candy searched her purse for tissues, with no luck. "Excuse me," she blubbered, running to the restroom.

She washed her face in cold water and took her time drying with paper towels. Maybe, if she delayed long enough, the cop would leave.

But he sat patiently waiting, tapping the eraser of the pencil on his crossed knee. When he saw Candy approaching, he stood up. "I'm sorry. I'm sure this must be trying for you."

"Have you heard anything about Sancho?"

"The doctor came out for a moment and said he'll be all right. That's all I know. Now," he readied his pencil over the pad, "back to the business at hand. What was that about it being our fault the man got hurt?"

"Exactly that. Someone's been vandalizing my house and stealing from me all along." She felt the tears again and sniffed. "It's ruining me, but what do you care?"

"Could you tell me exactly what time you found Mr. Gomez? And was he conscious?"

"At six o'clock this morning, barely conscious."

"You have no idea who could have attacked him?"

"None."

The cop licked his pencil again. "What about your workers? Did any of them have anything against Gomez?"

"Officer, he was attacked so someone could steal my appliances," Candy said, exasperated. "Appliances worth thousands of dollars."

The policeman shrugged. "You trust your crew, do you?"

"Implicitly."

"And you saw nothing to indicate who did it?"

Why did a picture of Chance's white van flash through her mind?

"No." She knew perfectly well Chance didn't do it. He would do anything for her, including lend her the money to pay off the exorbitant costs of the vandalism—and now the guy had started stealing! First her particleboard, now her appliances.

The doctor came down the hall, smiling. He held out his right hand to Candy. "I'm Dr. Holbrook, and you're Meez Candy?"

She laughed. "Yes, I'm Candy Hartwell. How's Sancho?"

"He's fine, and asking for you. You can go in for a few minutes."

Candy walked into Sancho's room. His head swathed in dressings, he looked as though he had done battle with tigers.

"I think I remember who hit me." He motioned toward his head. "If my head didn't hurt so loud I could tell you."

Candy's heart skipped a beat. She leaned over the man. "Was it someone you know?" she whispered.

He nodded. "I think so, but my head, she hurt so I can't think." He rested a moment. "I know who it was, Meez Candy," he finally said. "I just can't quite get it."

Suddenly, she couldn't handle anymore. "It's all right, Sancho. You just relax. Do you know how long you have to stay here?"

Sancho grinned broadly. "That doctor fellow nice. He fix me up good. But he say I have to stay all night. I'm ready to work, Meez Candy. You tell him I'm all right now."

Candy patted the dark hand she still held. "I certainly won't. The doctor fellow knows what's best for you. You just do as he says and you'll be back to work real soon." Her mind rushed back to Sancho's attack. She had to know who did it. "Now do you remember anything more about the man who attacked you?"

"I do. I know I do. I hear him come in front door so I say, 'Who's there?' He don't answer so I start into entryway. It was pitch dark, Meez Hartwell. The man grab me and spin me around with my back to him. Then he say something and all went black until you woke me. I almost remember."

Candy felt elation and dread battling inside her. Elation because they might be near an answer and dread because Sancho seemed so sure it was an acquaintance.

She patted Sancho's hand again. "You get some sleep, Sancho. And don't worry about a thing. We'll get this guy but it'll help if you can identify him."

Candy saw the officer sitting on the same chair, so she slipped the other way down the hall and out the door to freedom, then she went back to the house.

When she went inside the house, the men all gathered around. "Will he be all right?" Luke asked. "He's a pretty neat little guy."

"Neat like a scab," Slade grunted.

"Slade!" Candy flung at him. "Sancho's in the hospital, hurt."

"I don't care about that little Mexican, Candy, but I sure care about your appliances. What you gonna do now?"

"Well, you better care about Sancho. I intend to keep him on my crew as long as he'll stay. Now, some good news. Sancho almost remembers something that will tell us who our villain is. He thinks he knows him. He'll remember as soon as 'his head quits hurting so loud,' as he says."

Trumble grinned. "We may be bored to death after we catch

the guy."

"You may be bored but I'll be able to take a deep breath again. Well, I'm going to go call for more appliances."

What am I doing? Candy wondered as she hurried to use the phone at Chance's house. She couldn't pay for the appliances that were stolen. The store wouldn't sell more to her if they knew she had used all of her building loan.

Chance, still working on small jobs outside, glanced at Candy as she walked up to him, but continued screwing the shutter on.

"May I use your phone again, please?"

"Help yourself."

"Thanks. I have to reorder the appliances."

That got his attention. "What's wrong with the first ones?"

"Someone stole them."

Chance climbed down from his ladder and hurried to her side. "I thought we had that problem cured. Wasn't someone watching?"

Candy felt a lump growing in her throat. She simply couldn't break down again. Chance would think she had no guts at all. She swallowed twice before he pulled her head against his shoulder. After a few minutes, she lifted her face to his. "Not only am I going belly up," she said, "but Sancho could have been killed."

"What?" Chance pushed Candy to arm's length and searched her eyes. "What do you mean?"

"Could we sit down? I feel weak."

He tightened his arms a bit more and steered her to the tables. "What does Sancho have to do with anything?" he asked, after they were seated in the shade. He pulled off his blue-and-red flowered shirt and laid it across the end of the table.

"He was watching the house. Someone knocked him on the

head with something. He's in the hospital."

"I see." Chance's eyes narrowed to a squint. "Is he going to be all right?"

"Yes, but I'm giving it up, Chance. I can't go on any longer. I lived through my parents' deaths. I survived the years when I didn't know how to build. But I can't handle this violence. If you could give me my deposit on the next lots, I'd be glad to let you have them."

His jaw tightened. "You're not giving up—to me or anyone else. Get that through your head and keep it there."

Tears slid off Candy's nose onto the table. She brushed them away with the back of her hand. "My money's gone. I won't make enough on the house to pay for everything I've had to order twice. I won't even be able to start the next one and if I did, this – this horrible person would ruin it for me. Can't you see, Chance, he's not giving up until I quit."

Chance pulled her close and kissed her hair. "I hope you don't suspect me anymore."

"I don't know who I suspect. No, of course I don't. I just want to know who it is. Oh yes, I just remembered something. Sancho thinks it's someone he knows and thinks he'll remember when he's better."

Chance dropped his arms and sat up straight. "Don't tell a soul what you just told me, Candy. Not one soul in the world."

fifteen

Why would he instruct her not to tell anyone? And so definitively. "I already told my crew."

Chance lifted an eyebrow. "If we're dealing with the kind of person I think we are, that tidbit could be very dangerous to Sancho."

"Oh! He might do something to quiet Sancho." This was starting to sound like a bad movie. "But surely we're not dealing with a murderer. You're right, of course. Sancho could have been killed. But you don't suspect anyone on my crew, do you?"

He shrugged. "To quote a good friend, 'my brain's scrambled.' I guess I suspect everybody. Anyway, you'd better tell your crew that Sancho's forgotten everything." He chuckled. "Tell them the guy sounded like me, then he remembered the man was short."

"That sounds good. Maybe I'll say that. But if it's one of my crew, I can't trust them to guard the house."

"Sure you can. Nothing will ever happen when the guilty guy's on watch." Chance slid off the bench and helped Candy up. "Come on, let's go order more appliances."

As they stepped onto his porch, she looked up at Chance and said, "You know what gets me the most? This guy's never going to let me finish my house."

"I know." Chance had never sounded so sympathetic. "But, if you keep a continual guard, I think he'll give up."

Candy ordered the appliances and went back to her own house. Chance positively was not the one. He could never

136

have been so sympathetic and caring if he did it. Could he?
Did he need the money for his house sale as badly as she? She
really didn't know much about him, except that he lived in a
fantastic home.

She did too know! No one could be more honest than
Chance. And God had told her so repeatedly. "Lord," she
whispered, "You told me more than once that Chance isn't the
one. What's happened to my faith? I thought I walked close to
You—and had faith to spare. Help me, God. Help me never to
doubt You again." A Bible verse she had learned in church
kindergarten popped into her head. *Taste and see that the Lord
is good; blessed is the man who takes refuge in him.* (Psalm
34:8.) "Thank you, Lord," she said, out loud. Then she
giggled. "Would it be all right with you, Lord, if we made that
'blessed is the woman who trusts in Him?' "

The appliances were delivered before noon and Candy's
crew busily worked on installing them. At noon, Judy talked
after the men went back to work.

"Chance is getting better," she said.

Candy smiled, wryly. "I noticed. Do you think he's well
enough to bat someone over the head?"

Judy jumped up and started back to Chance's house. "That
dumb remark doesn't deserve an answer," she said, walking
away. "What's happening to the house is too bad, but you're
letting it ruin your life. Think about it, Candy—there's not
another Chance around the corner."

Candy shook her head. Right now Judy seemed to be the
big sister. And the wise one—and the one who had faith.

For a moment, Candy thought about her messed-up life.
One minute she knew for sure Chance would never do these
awful things and the next, she accused him. How could she do
that? Maybe she wasn't a Christian at all.

Clearing her mind, she went to the hospital to check on Sancho. "I see you're still on your back," she said walking into the room.

He grinned. "I feel great, Meez Candy, but they won't let me even sit up."

"Well, you do as they tell you. I want you back on the job soon."

"I will, but I don't like it. Anyway I have lots of times to think. In my mind I'm trying to see who hit me. I know him, Meez Candy. I know I do. He come out of the shadows soon."

"All right, Sancho, you keep trying, but listen to me. I have something very important to say to you."

His smile faded at her serious note. "You letting me go, Meez Candy?"

"Oh, Sancho, never. But listen. Chance told me to tell the guys on my crew that whatever you thought you remembered had all faded away and you can't remember anything. Understand?"

"You no want me remember?"

"I desperately want you to remember, Sancho. It may save my business—and your job. But Chance thinks it's dangerous for people to know you might identify your assailant. He might hurt you to keep you quiet." She squeezed his hand.

Sancho's eyes opened wide. "You mean he keel me?"

She giggled. "I think we're being ridiculous, Sancho, but let's keep it just between us, all right?"

"The police will ask."

"Of course you'll tell them." She held up crossed fingers. "And I pray God you do remember, Sancho. It's life and death, I'm afraid. My business life."

She went back to the house and told the men about her visit to Sancho and that he had realized he didn't know the man.

She went on to tell Chance's story, that he sounded like Chance but now Sancho realized the guy was much shorter. Buck swore softly under his breath. Luke and Slade looked angry.

The next day, Thursday, Candy took Sancho home to his trailer with instructions to stay inside and rest through the weekend. He could go back to work on Monday.

That night, Slade did guard duty. In the morning, Candy arrived with his breakfast and found out that everything had stayed in the house and in one piece. Slade seemed excited about finishing the house and thought the man would be afraid to return anymore after actually hurting someone.

At noon, Chance mouthed "wait a minute" to her as the crews went back to work. She settled back down, glad to spend a few minutes with him. "I'd like to have a party. Judy, Vic, you, and me. What do you think?"

His eyes showed strain—and love. He had never said he loved her but she knew he felt a lot, and though she felt a lot, too, she had done nothing but rebuff him.

Well, the time was right and she would love to spend some time with him. "I think it's a great idea. But Judy's been running around with Larry. I don't know if she even remembers Vic anymore."

As he reached for her hand, a small smile played on his lips. "I think she does. Will you help me?"

"I'd love to." Her fingers curled tightly around his hand. "What do you have in mind?"

He grinned openly. "Not much. Just a barbecue and swimming in my pool tomorrow or Sunday."

"Sounds wonderful. Would tomorrow be too soon?"

"Not for me. I'll check with Judy." He got up, walked

around the table and deposited a kiss on the top of her head. "I'm waiting for the day you learn to trust me."

Candy was, too. Every time she thought she had it all under control her traitorous mind insisted once more that Chance was the guilty man.

As he walked toward his house, Candy noticed how much better he was getting around. Hardly limped at all. She wondered if he'd be able to go into the water. She could almost feel the cool water in that huge pool right now.

The next day dawned clear, and by party time the sun shone hotly. Judy and Vic swam laps, raced, dived from both the low and high boards, tried to drown each other, then crawled out into the shade of the maple trees and weeping willows growing near the pool.

"Hungry?" Chance asked.

Judy dropped into a lawn chair. "I'm starved," she said. "I just swam ten laps—that must be at least ten miles. Plus all the other things we did. Bring on the food. If I don't replace the calories I used, I'll fade into nothing."

Vic looked her up and down. "Bring on the food. I don't want to change a thing about her."

Chance's eyes met Candy's and she went to him. "What can I do?"

He had prepared a table in the shade of the house. Plates, glasses, silverware, Doritos, Fritos, and several kinds of potato chips already graced the table.

He washed his hands with a moist towel and lifted the barbecue lid. Four foil-wrapped potatoes sat on the grill, tiny puffs of steam escaping through the folds. Several browning ears of corn took up more space. As Candy watched him place four large steaks on the grill, she realized she felt hungry too.

He lowered the lid, then put both arms over her shoulders and leaned his forehead onto hers. "You can transfer everything in the refrigerator to the table out here. I'll check on the steaks. They don't take long."

When Candy opened the refrigerator, she found a colorful tossed salad of red tomatoes and radishes, orange carrots, purple cabbage, and all shades of green vegetables—lettuce, peppers, spinach, cucumbers, celery. She pulled the salad and two kinds of dressing out and carried them to the table. Then, she found two dips for the chips, sour cream dressing for the potatoes, and a small potato salad.

"There. What a meal," she said.

He looked the table over. "Did you find the pop?"

When she returned with the pop, the steaks, corn, and potatoes sat on individual plates, steaming. The hungry people dug in almost before Chance added the "Amen" to the blessing. Candy couldn't stop until she felt overstuffed.

"Time to crank up the ice cream freezer," Chance said after everyone slowed to a stop.

"Could we take a rain check?" Vic asked. "I'm already grossly overfed. Besides, we promised each other we'd take a drive up into the Blues." Vic shook hands with Chance. "Thanks for a great day."

"You're welcome. If you get home early, come back here and we'll make the ice cream tonight." He glanced at Candy. "Can you still be here?"

"Sure. I don't have any deadlines today."

"Did you decide to swim?" Chance asked as the young people drove away.

"No, I'll wait for you."

He took her hand and started toward the door. "Let's go enjoy the air conditioning then."

"What do you think about Vic and Judy?" she asked, after they had settled down at a small table in the basement.

"Looks good to me. I don't think she even remembers Larry's name."

"Don't you believe it. She'll be running off with him tomorrow night and coming home at dawn. Her actions upset me more than my house problems do."

He shook his head. "I think Judy's much more mature than you give her credit for. But, if I could do anything to stop it, I would. All of it." He picked up the cards. "Want to get creamed in a game of gin rummy?"

Candy won three games in a row.

"Okay, I'm a believer," he said. "A woman can do anything as well as a man and probably better."

"Cards don't prove anything, but shall I let you win, once?"

He extended his hands imploringly. "Please. Just once would help preserve my masculine ego." Then a new look came over his face. "Do you still suspect me of being your vandal, Candy? I guess now we say vandal and thief, don't we, since the guy's enlarged his activities."

"N–n–no–o–o, I don't suspect you." That didn't come out very convincingly, even to her. "Of course, I don't," she said.

He reached for her hand. "But you lack a lot of being sure."

Why did this subject ever get started? She so wanted a perfect afternoon. "I don't know. I don't know anything anymore, but let's don't let it wreck our day, Chance. In my heart I know you couldn't be the one. And God's assured me a million times. But my faith gets weak when my head reminds me of all the things that point to you. Then, I come to my senses and know it isn't you." She stopped and grinned. "Please don't ask me to make sense."

Pity replaced wariness in his eyes. He got up from the game

table and led her to a couch then pulled her down with him and gathered her into his arms. "I understand," he said against her hair.

A moment later, he released her and she felt breathless. The only thing she felt certain about right now was her love for the big man beside her. Finally, she became aware that he was gazing at her.

"You do care, don't you, love?" he whispered.

"I care. Oh, Chance, I care so much."

He didn't touch her but continued to gaze into her eyes. "I'm beginning to understand. You're afraid to fall in love with someone who's ruining you."

She nodded then shook her head. "Not quite, but I have to solve my mystery before I can do anything. Anything at all. My friend is not only causing me to lose the house I'm building but the one Judy and I live in. And besides all that, he's making me crazy." She tumbled against him and his arms hesitated only a moment before holding her loosely. Just then, the telephone rang.

"I don't hear a thing," he said.

"Neither do I." Immediately, a picture of Judy and Vic popped into her mind. Blood dripped from Judy's face and dirt covered her clothes. She jumped from Chance's arms and grabbed the telephone.

"Mr. Chancellor, please," the voice said.

She handed him the phone and he raised an eyebrow at her. "Yes? When? Call the police. We'll be right there."

He jumped to his feet. "Come on," he said, moving toward the front door, "someone's messing with your house."

On the road, he explained. "It was one of the land developers preparing your new lots. He saw someone and tried to call you. Not reaching you, he tried me." He took his eyes from the road and looked quizzically at her. "Did you have a vision? You jumped after that phone like it was a life and death matter."

She grinned. "As a matter of fact I did, only the vision was of Judy and Vic in a wreck." She thought a moment. "Hurry, please. When we catch the guilty guy my whole life will fall into place."

In a few minutes he turned in to the building sites. As Chance braked, lights flashed atop two police cars. They hopped out and ran to Candy's house.

sixteen

Candy and Chance found two police officers, each restraining a struggling man. "What's going on, officers?" Chance asked. "What were they doing?"

"Killing each other," one of the cops said, heaving breathlessly. The officer held the man's arms down as he thrashed from side to side.

Candy finally saw the man's face and couldn't believe her eyes! "What are you doing here, Wright? I hope they throw you in jail forever."

He glared at her. "I should've let the bum wreck your house."

Candy followed Wright's angry bloodshot eyes to the other man and found Pete Meyer struggling with the other officer.

"I knew it!" she screamed. "Somewhere deep inside I've known it was that guy all the time. What are you doing here, anyway?"

Pete looked sullen. "I just came around looking for a job and that jerk came on like a grizzly bear."

"He did not," Wright bellowed. "I seen him peeking in the windows. Anyone who peeks in windows'll do most anything."

Chance sighed. "They may as well release them, don't you think, Candy?"

"No way," she said. "Pete's threatened me more than once. We've found our man."

One of the officers asked Candy to tell them about her experience with Pete Meyer. "We know he didn't do anything this time," the officer said when she finished. "I have to tell you it's been so long it won't be easy to pin anything on him. But the next time something happens he'll be our first suspect."

Just what she would have expected from these cops. "Okay, turn them loose," she said.

"Did you hear these kind people?" one officer said to Wright.

Wright gave a mighty twist, but remained constrained in the man's arms. "I heard. Turn me loose."

The officer tightened his hold until Wright winced. "I'm not turning anyone loose until you promise to get off the premises immediately with no violence. Meaning leave Meyer alone. Got it?" He turned to the other policeman. "Turn him loose," he said, nodding at Pete Meyer.

The other officer slowly relaxed his hold on Meyer who took off down the street. The policeman holding Wright grinned, then released him. Wright gingerly stepped away from the cop, dusted off his dirty, torn garments where the policeman had touched him, picked up his hat from the ground, tipped it at Candy, then strolled off in a leisurely fashion.

Candy started giggling, breaking the tension.

Chance chuckled then guffawed until the policemen joined in.

"I don't know," one of the officers said, "was it really this funny?"

"Not really," Candy choked through her laughter. "It's just that we're trying so hard to find who's destroying my house, then we catch those two."

Chance took Candy's elbow. "Let's get back to what we were doing." His look told Candy reams about his feelings for her.

"Shall we try gin rummy again?" he asked, unlocking the front door.

She walked past him and collapsed on the couch. "Maybe we could just talk. I feel as exhausted as if I'd been in that fracas myself."

Chance sat on the rocker, peering into Candy's face. "Did I tell you I love you? I want you to know. It might make a difference."

Candy scooted to the end of the sofa where she could reach him and took his hand in both of hers. "Thank you, Chance. It means everything because I love you, too. God keeps telling me that you aren't the one, too. And I know for sure you didn't do it."

He moved to the sofa and scooped her into his lap. "You have to believe. I've been wild for you ever since you decided I was trying to steal your lots. Now that I think about it, you've always thought I was stealing something from you or doing something equally awful."

The doorbell rang, then Judy and Vic walked in.

Candy slid off Chance's lap to the couch beside him, still leaning on him.

Vic sat in the rocker and pulled Judy onto his lap. "We kept thinking about homemade ice cream and you two here without anyone to chaperone you, so we went only to Tollgate."

Chance gently disentangled himself from Candy, stood to his feet, and pulled her up. "I hear the freezer calling."

She followed him to the kitchen, pulled the already-mixed ice cream from the refrigerator, and poured it into the freezer while he put in the salt and ice.

"There," he said, "it can do the work while we bother Judy and Vic. We'll check it in thirty minutes."

The ice cream turned out rich and creamy. "I've never tasted homemade ice cream before," Vic said, filling his third bowl, "but I intend to have it again." He smiled tenderly at Judy. "We'll have to get a freezer."

"What do you think of Vic?" Candy asked Judy later that evening.

Judy cocked her head. "He's really nice—for a kid."

"Won't you please quit with Larry and just go with Vic?"

Judy shook her head. "No way. Larry's grown up."

Candy went to her room feeling depressed and took her Bible from the shelf. "Please lead me to a verse that will encourage me, Lord," she said aloud. She opened to the Psalms. *Those who know your name will trust in you, for you, Lord, have never forsaken those who seek you.* (Psalm 9:10) She reread the verse and felt strength flow into her body. God hadn't forsaken her—she had forsaken Him. "Help me, Lord," she cried, "help me to trust in You. And protect Judy while she's being foolish."

Then, she felt impressed to turn the pages of her Bible again. A moment later, another verse met her gaze. *In God, whose word I praise, in God I trust; I will not be afraid. What can mortal man do to me?* (Psalm 56:4) She couldn't believe it. Now God was encouraging her about her house. "Dear Lord in heaven," she whispered, "I think I could be unafraid if I only knew who's doing this dreadful thing." Immediately, she felt a strong guilt. "I'm sorry, Father. All I need to know is who it isn't. And I know it isn't Chance. Help me believe, Lord, and thank You."

When Candy took Luke's breakfast at six o'clock the next morning she noticed Chance's beat-up van. *Oh, oh, I hope everything's all right at my house*, she thought. Then she scolded herself. What was the matter with her? But she felt strong faith this morning. Maybe accusing Chance was just a bad habit she had acquired.

Everything was all right but Candy smelled alcohol as she and Luke ate. "The carpets are coming today," she said, draining her coffee mug. "We'll have to keep a special watch until they're down."

He nodded, shoving in the last bite of his toast and bacon sandwich. "I know. We'll watch every minute."

After putting the breakfast things in the car, she returned to the house. Chance joined her. "Everything all right?" he asked.

She thought a moment. "With the house, yes. With me, I'm not sure. I may be losing it mentally. When I saw your van so early this morning the first thing I thought was what's missing now."

He stiffened.

"I'm sorry. I care far too much for you to hurt you, but I want you to know my mental state."

Chance took her in his arms. "You're all right. I don't want to hear any more talk like that." He kissed her but released her immediately. "What's going on at your house today?" he asked.

She sighed. "Carpets are going in at my house today. I wish they could all be installed in one day. I'm scared silly my visitor's going to get them."

"Just be sure you have someone on guard at all times." After a moment his expression changed into a smile. "We're exactly together now. My carpets are coming today, too."

"And mine better sell quick. But I'm not worrying. God tells us not to worry about tomorrow." She grinned. "Well, you'll have to give me credit for trying."

When the carpet mechanics arrived, she asked them how long it would take. They said they hoped to be finished by Friday.

The men started work and Candy went about her duties. Her men worked outside installing the underground sprinkling system. She filled in the nail holes in the window and door casings.

As she worked, Chance appeared again. "I can't seem to get going. Put that stuff down and come talk to me." He took her hand then led her outside to the tables.

They sat down together. "At least we're talking now," he said. "I've decided I'd rather you'd tell me you think I'm a rotten crook than to refuse to talk to me." He grinned and pulled her close.

She leaned on his shoulder, wrapping both arms around his left one. "I'd rather talk, too. I know you wouldn't hurt anyone and especially not me because you love me. But my mind blows a fuse sometimes and I lose control. I'm trying."

He tapped her nose with his right index finger. "Really trying, huh? Well, would you like to drive over to Walla Walla Saturday night and try a play at Cordiner Hall? Then dinner?"

Candy felt so light she thought she would take off and fly. "Thanks, this will give me something to look forward to besides my night visitor. I read they're going to be showing a really funny comedy."

Later that afternoon, Candy went shopping. A new outfit would make her night out extra special. After going through several shops, she found exactly what she wanted. She luxuriated in the soft swish as the royal blue satin dress slipped over her shoulders and fell in lovely folds to the floor.

The clerk zipped it up the back and Candy walked to a full-length mirror. She gasped as she saw how beautiful the dress looked on her. The fitted waist made her tiny body look minuscule. Small bows, created from the same fabric, covered the elasticized shoulder seams and flared over the sleeves. The same pert bows wandered around the hem, giving it a little extra weight.

The clerk left for a moment and returned with a pair of lace gloves in the same electric color, and dainty matching pumps. Candy took them in her hands, turning them over and over. A moment later, she smiled into the clerk's eyes. "Now, all I need is an evening bag."

The clerk produced a tiny white beaded bag, trimmed in exactly the same blue. "This dress was truly made for you, Miss Hartwell," she said.

"I can't disagree with you," Candy said, feeling light and happy. *I'm a fool to spend the money*, she told herself, but she said something entirely different to the clerk. "I'm not even asking the price. Just put it on this card." She handed over her only credit card, the one had promised herself to use only for identification. How much could a new outfit cost compared with the astronomical bills she had accumulated over the last few weeks?

The week went by in a whirl with the men taking turns staying in the house at night. Sancho had come back to work Monday and worked as hard as usual.

On Friday, Candy left work at four o'clock, nearly forgetting her worries. The carpet men had finished the last room so she hoped the night visitor had struck for the last time.

The next evening she took her time dressing, putting her dark curls on top of her head with short tendrils curling around her face. When she finished putting on her makeup, she looked at herself carefully. Her eyes seemed even larger than usual, she noticed, but thought how beautiful it would be if they were blue instead of brown so they could match her lovely new dress. Her high cheekbones looked exquisitely dainty, and quiet pink lip gloss made her mouth warm but innocent. An electric blue clematis over her right ear completed her look.

After a touch of heady perfume, she picked up her sparkling evening bag and stepped into the living room.

"Can!" Judy jumped up from her chair. Running to Candy she looked down at her in amazement. "Can, are you in there?"

Candy laughed. "I'm here."

Judy hugged her, carefully not mussing anything. "You're positively gorgeous. I'm predicting you come home engaged."

Candy smiled her thanks. "I don't even know what I hope for at this point. I just want to have a fairy tale evening and forget my troubles." She smiled up at her little sister. "Of course, I'm open to a surprise ending if things go just right."

Chance's Bronco pulled into the driveway at seven o'clock and Judy, signaling Candy to step back into the center of the room, opened the door.

When he saw her his mouth formed an *O*, but no sound came forth. He shifted the small box he held from one hand to the other, his eyes darting from her eyes to the dress to her eyes to the gloves. After an eternity, he stepped over to her. "I have no breath to describe you," he whispered in a raw husky voice. "And if I did, the English language wouldn't do the job." Awkwardly, he handed her the florist's box from which she withdrew a lovely gardenia wrist corsage. Handing the corsage back to him, she extended her wrist.

As he fastened it, she noticed his blond hair looked like

golden sunshine against the beautiful black tuxedo. The maroon bow tie and cummerbund and the white ruffled shirt made him look like a fairy tale prince. *Her* Prince Charming. She took a deep breath and inhaled his spicy aftershave. "The corsage is beautiful and just the right color." She stood on tiptoe and kissed his lips. "Thank you," she squeaked. To add the final glamorous touch, she noticed his eyes had turned an extra brilliant blue, matching her dress exactly.

"Well, listen up," Judy said brightly.

"The fairy tale princess, going out for the night,
The fairy tale prince will do everything right.
He'll ask her to marry, his love o'er her pour
They'll wed and live happily, forevermore."

Judy's poem snapped them out of their daze. "We're leaving," Chance answered. "May I?" He held out his arm for Candy and steered her toward the door as if he feared she would break.

"Do you mind if we eat after the play?" he asked as he negotiated the evening traffic and turned west onto the highway. "I don't want to rush anything tonight."

"Not at all. Tonight I'm a young girl on her first date, without a problem in the world. All I'm going to worry about is which fork to use first." She lifted her wrist and inhaled the heady gardenia fragrance.

At her words, his hands relaxed visibly on the steering wheel. "Great. We're in our teens and on our first date." Five minutes after leaving the highway, he pulled into the parking lot across the street from Cordiner Hall, which was filling in spite of the fact that it was just thirty minutes before curtain time.

Chance led Candy down the aisle to the reserved seats and to the middle of the row. As they sat down, Candy realized what a wonderful view she would have. After this ostentatious beginning, she wondered where they would eat—and what.

Then she wondered how the evening would end. How did she hope it would end? She honestly didn't know. One thing she did know—she loved Chance and if he should turn out to be her night visitor, she would have a broken heart to heal. But what was she thinking? She knew better then to even let that kind of thought surface anymore. She had resurrected her faith and wouldn't lose it again.

In a little while the play started, completely immersing her in the hilarious make-believe world portrayed before her. About forty-five minutes into the play an usher approached them. "Mr. Chancellor?"

"Yes?"

"Sorry to disturb you, sir, but I believe there's a telephone call for the lady. Candy Hartwell?"

Candy's heart stood still. "Yes. I'll come."

He stood up. "Who knows we're here?" he whispered into her ear.

"Judy. Something's happened to her."

He followed her to the phone that she snatched to her ear. "Hello, Judy, are you all right? Oh, no! Where is he now? Are you there? All right, I'm on my way. See you in a minute."

She looked into Chance's eyes. "Take it easy," he said steering her out the door.

"Where to?" he asked after starting the car.

She put her fingers to her throat. "Mountain View General Hospital. Sancho's been run down and isn't going to live. Chance, it's my fault."

His lips tightened into a narrow line. He said nothing until he parked at the hospital. Then he pulled her to him. "It's not your fault," he said tenderly. "You had nothing to do with it and it may not even be connected with anything." Releasing her, he climbed out and locked his door, then helped her out. "Chin up, love. I'm with you."

Vic and Judy met them at the door and led them to the emergency room. Candy momentarily wondered why Vic was there.

As they walked, Judy hugged her. "Can, I didn't know what to do. I couldn't bear to ruin your special evening."

"You did the right thing," Chance said.

"They said he was asking for you, Can. That's why I finally called. They told me to find you if I possibly could, that he wanted to tell you something important."

"He probably knows who did it," Candy said in a taut voice.

"Miss Hartwell?" A nurse asked, as they approached the desk.

"Yes." She hardly recognized her own voice. "How is he?"

The nurse shook her head. "Not good at all. He has extensive injuries. Fortunately, he was wearing a helmet. Otherwise, he'd have been killed instantly."

Candy gasped. "He was on his cycle?"

The nurse nodded. "The police said the motorcycle looked like smashed tin cans. And the driver didn't stop." She shook her head in disbelief. "He's asking for you, Miss Hartwell. You'd better go in for a few minutes."

With dread, Candy followed the uniformed woman through the double doors then down the hall. Sancho looked small beneath the sheet with several machines and paraphernalia attached to him. Once again, she took his brown hand in hers. "Hi, Sancho, it's Candy."

His eyes looked sunken but he tried to smile. "He get me, Meez Candy."

"The same man who took my appliances?"

"Yes."

"What was he driving, Sancho?"

"White van. It was him."

White van! She swallowed twice. "Okay, Sancho, you take it easy and get well now. You probably shouldn't talk anymore."

She released his hand but he reached for her almost frantically. "No, Meez Candy, I know who—" His hand dropped and his eyes fluttered shut as his voice faded away.

Candy ran from the room directly into the nurse who stood outside. "Go check him, quick."

The nurse ran in and two doctors followed. Candy plopped down beside Chance in the waiting room.

"What happened?" Judy asked.

Candy lifted horror-filled eyes to Judy. "I don't know," she sniffled. "He said it was the same man who got the appliances." Then to Chance, "I think he knows for sure now who the man is. And he was driving a white van."

He sighed. "Thank God I was with you."

They rested quietly until a policeman approached them. "Miss Hartwell?"

Candy heaved a monstrously audible sigh. "Yes." Then she stood to her full five feet. "Please, tell us what happened."

He took out his pad and scanned it. "Sancho Gomez was run down by unknown person or persons at approximately five o'clock this evening." He studied his pad a moment and continued. "There were no witnesses but Gomez says it was a white van and keeps saying he knows the driver." He looked at Candy with a raised eyebrow. "Says he can't tell anyone but you."

A white van—and he was hit at five o'clock—two hours before Chance picked her up. And Sancho knows the man. No! She couldn't think like that! "Where did it happen?" she choked out.

He checked his pad again. "On Stone Mill highway about a mile south of the Oregon border. Gomez had apparently just entered the highway from an abandoned trailer there." He shook his head. "May have pulled out in front of the van."

"I don't think so, Officer. I'm guessing the van was waiting for him." She sank back into her chair.

The officer chose the chair next to her and sat down. "Why would you say a thing like that?"

Candy pulled in a long breath. Why should she go over it all again for the police? "Because he thinks it's the same man who knocked him over the head about ten days ago while he watched my house."

The policeman's head jerked around. "Did you report this incident?"

Candy felt like twisting his long nose. "Of course, we reported it—for all the good it did. We've reported numerous incidents."

The police officer scrutinized his pad, ignoring her complaints. "The bike was totaled," he volunteered, "but we found white paint on it, verifying Gomez's story about the vehicle."

Chance leaned forward in his seat to see the policeman. "What did the doctor say about his injuries?"

"Said his chances were slim to nil, as I recall." His eyes wandered down the hall behind Chance. "Here he comes now."

All five people met the doctor. "Why don't we go sit down

and talk?" he said. He led them into a small room with a table in the center, surrounded by six black leather-and-chrome chairs. They all sat around the doctor.

"I think we're going to operate," he said, grimly. "His injuries are so extensive it's hard to know what to do, but we're finding he's surprisingly tough. His pelvis is broken. Both legs have multiple fractures. And there are undetermined internal injuries." He shrugged. "His chances of survival are so slight we hesitate to put him through the trauma."

"He's tough, Doctor. Please try." Candy's liquid brown eyes pleaded as eloquently as her words.

The police officer cleared his throat. "I suppose he isn't able to answer questions?"

The doctor looked sharply at the man in blue. "You already had a shot at him. It's our turn now."

The policeman got up. "Fair enough. Good luck, Doctor. I'll check in the morning."

As the officer left the room, Candy sighed.

The doctor looked around at the four remaining. "Why don't you all go home," he suggested quietly. "Mr. Gomez isn't going to die right now. Neither are we necessarily going to operate immediately. We may play the waiting game for a few hours."

Vic got up and pulled Judy up beside him. "Let's go get some rest." He turned to the others. "What about you?"

"I don't know," Candy said. "You two go on. And thanks again." The two younger people waved and walked away wearily.

The doctor started toward the door. "I'm going to check on him again. If you like, I'll have another report in about thirty minutes."

"Thank you, Doctor. Shall we wait here?"

"That'll be fine." He shut the door, leaving Chance and Candy alone.

Candy cradled her head in her arms on the table. *Please, Father,* she prayed silently, *help Sancho get well. This isn't his fault and he shouldn't have to suffer. And please help him to tell us who ran him down. I don't want to know but I have to. Thank you, in Jesus' name.* In a moment, she felt Chance's arm over her shoulders. Neither said a word. Then he stood behind her, silently kneading the muscles in her neck and shoulders. It felt so good she hoped he would never quit.

After several minutes, he sat back down beside Candy. "Let's pray for Sancho," he said taking her hand in his. Then he prayed a simple sincere prayer asking for healing for the broken little man.

Forty minutes later, the door opened and the doctor came in again. "Miss Hartwell, Mr. Gomez is conscious and demanding to see you. He's quite agitated, so you'd better go quickly."

On her feet in a flash, Candy followed the man into Sancho's room. She ran quickly to his bed and leaned over. "I'm here, Sancho," she said. "Candy. Did you want to tell me something?"

His glazed eyes searched Candy's. "Yes, Meez Candy, I tell you his name," he said clearly. "I know him. You know him, too." His attention wandered and his voice faded away.

Candy leaned closer. "Sancho, please tell me."

No response.

"Please, Sancho, think!"

Trying to rally he spoke again, faintly this time. "You like him. I didn't think he. . . ."

seventeen

"Sancho, you have to tell me." Candy restrained herself from shaking the broken man. "Do something," she begged the doctor, standing beside her. "What he was telling me was important."

The doctor examined Sancho. "He's slipped back into a coma. He won't be saying anything until—or unless—he regains consciousness," he said, propelling her toward the door. "You may as well go back to your friend. And I do understand the importance of finding the person who did this grisly thing."

Chance met her at the door and helped her to a chair. "What did Sancho say?" he asked.

She raised stricken eyes. "He knows who did it, but lost consciousness before he could tell me."

"He'll wake and tell someone in a little while," he said as she laid her head back on her arms.

She looked at him with round eyes again. "I'm sitting right here until he regains consciousness. Why don't you go on home?"

"Not a chance." He stood behind her, kneading her neck muscles again.

After a long while, she raised her head. Tears bubbled over the edge of her eyes. "Sancho is so special. I don't want him to die."

The doctor arrived so quietly he reached the table before they knew he was in the room. Candy jumped up. "Does he want me? What's going on?"

The kindly doctor restrained Candy and pushed her back into her chair. "Sit down, Miss Hartwell. Gomez is in surgery. That man has tremendous spirit. He's refused to die, so we're doing our best to help him live."

"How long?" Candy asked, touching his arm.

The doctor sat silent a few moments. "Most of the night, I imagine. If he makes it through surgery, he'll be unconscious for another twenty-four hours. We have your number, Miss Hartwell, so there's no point in your hanging around."

Chance stopped the car at Candy's house, walked her to the front door, and kissed her lightly on the forehead. "Good night, love," he whispered. "Try to get some sleep."

The clock said two-fifteen when Candy slipped between the sheets, too weary to remove her makeup. She whispered a prayer for her Father to be with Sancho during the long surgery and for his complete healing.

"Can," Judy shook Candy's shoulders gently, "it's the hospital."

Candy bolted upright, draped a light robe over her shoulders, and raced to the phone. "Candy Hartwell. He did? Great. That is good news, isn't it? That long? Okay, I will. Thanks a lot, Doctor."

"Tell me, Can." Judy asked eagerly.

"He said Sancho made it through surgery, his vital signs are momentarily stable, but it'll be forty-eight hours before they know anything. And for me to stick by the phone."

Before Candy reached her room, the phone rang again. "Hi, Chance. He's alive, but it'll be a while before they know if he's going to make it. What? You really think I should? Okay."

"Judy," she said, "Chance wants us to tell everyone there's no hope for Sancho. He's going to tell his crew the same story, which is almost true."

Judy looked puzzled then shrugged. "Okay. I won't say a word." She started out then turned back. "Wait a minute. It seems fair that Vic should know, since he was with us last night. Can I tell him?"

Candy smiled at her sometimes grownup little sister. "Of course. Just tell him it's very private. I'm curious, Judy, how did Vic happen to be at the hospital with you?"

Judy looked embarrassed. "I needed someone, Can. I really did. And Larry wasn't the one." She smiled and shrugged prettily.

Candy laughed. "Great. I'm happy about that. Just one more thing. Please don't say anything to Larry about any hope for Sancho."

Judy agreed and left.

Candy put some bread in the toaster and pulled the orange juice from the refrigerator. She hardly ever missed church but she didn't dare leave this morning. When she asked God to bless her food, she also thanked Him for helping Sancho this far and pleaded for Him to heal the plucky little man.

She relaxed and finally faced her thoughts. Chance drove a white van to work every day. And his typewriter's printing matched the awful note. And many more things entered her head. She closed her eyes and asked her Heavenly Father to show her once more if Chance was innocent. As she sat quietly waiting, she remembered how unhappy he'd been when he found her carrying nails and staples. And he'd told her how to cover the red paint after one bout of vandalism. And how he insisted she have guys to stay and watch the house. And how he was always more than willing to take his turn. And he loved her.

Suddenly, her heart felt lighter and she thought she heard

soft music. After the music ended, she waited a few silent minutes then took a shower. After showering, she dressed in a top and jeans. When she came out, she found Chance at the front door.

"I missed you," he said, kissing her on the cheek. "Can we go somewhere? I have great news."

"I have to wait here for the doctor's call. But tell me the news." They sat down at the kitchen table with steaming cups of coffee.

"I just came from our houses, where I caught a real estate agent showing them to a very interested couple."

She grabbed his arm. "Interested in which house?"

As he laughed into her eyes, she felt her heart growing so large it would have to escape its confines. Finally, she consciously willed herself to concentrate on the house. "Which house are they interested in?" she repeated softly.

"Exactly what I've been telling you. They will look at both houses."

"What did they say?"

He grinned as though enjoying the game. "I had a minute alone with the realtor and she told me they're unbelievable prospects—cash money and they've narrowed the choice to ours—so one of us has sold a house."

Candy's heart raced differently this time. Cash buyers. No wait for credit. She could have her money inside a week and be home free. Well, not exactly free. She still had to pay all the extra money this house had cost, then pay off one of her lots to build on the next. She had planned to use the profit from this house to do that but there wouldn't be any profit now. Just a big loss. She couldn't even bear to wonder how she and Judy would live.

"Hey, are you still there?" Chance tapped her head gently.

"Oh. I was thinking about my good luck. At this point a quick sale's all I could ask for. God's on the job after all."

He chuckled. "You haven't sold it, yet."

Her chin went out. "They'll buy mine, just you wait. My circular staircase and round wall will do it."

"I have an idea," Chance said, getting up. "Let's go to the hospital and check on Sancho. It'll do us good to get out."

"He's doing remarkably well," the nurse on duty said in response to their question. "I mean just to be alive after what he's gone through."

Chance rubbed his chin thoughtfully. "Could you tell us what they did?"

The nurse shook her head. "No, but the surgeon will be along pretty soon, if you'd care to wait."

"I'll get us some coffee." Chance's long legs strode off down the hall.

While Candy waited, she tuned in to the nurse who was talking on the telephone. "I'm sorry I can't give out any information except to his family. His father? Oh, I'm sorry, Mr. Gomez. Your son is listed in critical but momentarily stable condition. I can't tell you yet. It will be at least thirty-six hours before the doctor will know anything."

Candy jumped up and ran to the desk, signaling frantically. "Please, I must talk to that man."

The nurse nodded at Candy. "Just a moment, Mr. Gomez, someone here wants to speak to you."

Candy took the phone but only a dial tone buzzed into her ear. Another dead end!

Chance put a coffee-filled paper cup into her hand. "Drink that, love," he said.

"Chance, someone who claimed to be Sancho's father

called, but hung up before I could talk to him."

He steered her to a seat. "Now let me get this straight," he said. "Sancho's father called—just like that. How did he know Sancho was hurt? Where did he call from?"

"I don't know. Let's go ask the nurse."

The nurse thought a moment. "Uh, he didn't say, but sounded local as far as I could tell."

Chance looked at Candy.

She shook her head. "No way. He doesn't have anyone here." Tears welled into her eyes. "Except me. He has only me."

Chance stood quietly a moment, leaning on the desk. Then he snapped his fingers, turning to the nurse again. "Did he speak with a heavy Mexican accent?"

The nurse stuck out her lower lip in deep thought, then shook her head. "Not that I could notice."

"Report that call to the police," Chance yelled. "That was the guy who ran Sancho down."

An officer came to the hospital immediately, but the nurse couldn't tell him anything she hadn't told Chance and Candy.

As they talked, the surgeon came in. "Did someone here wish to talk to me?" he asked the group in general.

Candy waved her hand. "I do, Doctor."

He came over and shook hands with her. "I'm Dr. Zane."

Chance draped a long arm over Candy's shoulder. "I'm Jeremy Chancellor and this is Sancho's boss, Candy Hartwell."

Dr. Zane stuck his hands into his white coat pockets. "By all the rules I go by, Mr. Gomez should be dead, but he's a fighter."

"Can you tell us what you did?"

The doctor hesitated, then nodded. "Sure, I'll try. We took

out some intestine, removed the bone splinters from his legs, and did what we had to do to fix them. And put the pelvis together as best we could."

Chance whistled. "He has an uphill road, doesn't he?"

The doctor nodded, then shook his head slowly.

"But what do you think, Doctor? Can he make it?" Candy gritted her teeth waiting for the answer.

"My answer is an almost positive no, but I also guaranteed he wouldn't live through surgery. Then I said he couldn't make it through the night, so what do I know?" He pointed skyward with his thumb. "I guess Gomez will live until He says otherwise."

Chance delivered Candy home, saying he had something he had to do.

How am I supposed to sit here and wait? she asked herself. Wait for news of Sancho. Wait for news from the realtor. Wait for Judy. Wait for Chance. Where did he go, anyway?

Chance didn't return, the hospital didn't call, and neither did the realtor. Judy was gone all day, too. It seemed that at least Judy could be there for her when she needed someone.

Candy looked up all the Bible verses about praying for healing, and prayed for Sancho accordingly. Then she prayed for her dear Father to watch over Judy and the house she was trying to build, and to lead in her friendship with Chance. She went to bed at ten o'clock. Exhausted from the night before, she dropped off to sleep and awakened at five o'clock in the morning, alert and ready to go.

Creeping quietly from her room, she called the hospital. Sancho still lived! "Thank You, Father," she said aloud. That seemed to be all she could ask for at this moment.

The phone rang before she went to work. Candy answered,

fearful it might be the hospital, but a cheery voice spoke. "This is Reva. I need to see you right away."

Ten minutes later, Reva sat in Candy's living room. "If you can have your house ready by Wednesday, you have a sale."

Candy mentally went over her house. "I can have it ready. All I lack inside is hanging doors and some trim. Outside, a swing is to be hung in the patio. We can do that Wednesday without bothering the movers at all. How's that?"

The real estate lady moved toward the kitchen table. "Great. Let's sign the papers and I'll take off."

Candy noticed an unusual phrase in the contract: *"This agreement null and void if property not ready for buyers Wednesday, August 26."* No problem, she'd have it ready, easy.

Chance dropped by after supper and they played gin rummy. "How come you're all smiles tonight?" he asked after he won his second game. "Did you win the lottery?"

"Almost." She hadn't decided whether to tell him, but she could hardly hold back when he asked. "The people are buying my place. Please don't be unhappy. I needed the sale more than you."

He laid his cards down. "Gin," he said, then grinned and got up. "I have to go. Of course I'm glad they bought yours. You needed a miracle and that's exactly what this is. Congratulations." With a wave, he hurried out the door.

"That was strange," Judy said, looking up from her stitchery.

"What?"

"His leaving without waiting for you to walk him to the car. And he didn't even kiss you goodbye."

"Yes, I guess it was strange, but he's pleased by my sale."

"Haven't you learned yet, Can?" Judy said through a

mouthful of embroidery floss. "People never mean what they say."

About dawn the next morning, Candy, still yawning, approached the new house with Luke's breakfast. She had come extra early to get a good start on the work that had to be finished tonight.

As she turned into her driveway she saw a tall man running to a white van that was backed up to her house. As he jumped into the rig she recognized Chance's red-and-blue flowered shirt.

Although she gave a couple of quick honks in greeting, the van tore past her so quickly that she didn't get even a glimpse of him. Wonder what he's doing out so early, she thought as she gathered up Luke's breakfast and went into her house.

Luke sprawled on his cot in the utility room, surrounded by beer cans. Feeling uneasy, she stepped around the rank-smelling man and went into the entryway. She started up the stairs but recoiled in horror. The carpeting was gone! She ran up the stairs to find bare floors in the living room and dining room. There wasn't one carpet left in the entire house! Even the pads were gone!

"Wake up, you fool," she screamed as she returned to Luke. "You slept while the carpets were being stolen!" She slammed his cot over, dumping him onto the cold utility room floor.

Pulling his legs into a comfortable position, he slept on, reeking of alcohol. He didn't stir even when she shook him hard.

"Get out of my house!" she screamed. "And never come back!"

Still, he didn't move.

She ran outside and filled a small bucket with water. "Luke, get out of my house," she yelled at the top of her lungs.

He didn't stir.

"Get out," she said, giving him one more chance. "Okay, you asked for it!" She poured the cold water over his head.

He jerked violently, then sat up, trying to focus on Candy.

"You're leaving," she screamed into his ear. "Get out!" As she tried to push him toward the door, Slade rushed in.

He looked from Candy to Luke. "What's happenin'?" he asked.

"He's leaving, that's what's happening." She tugged on the stuporous man but he was dead weight. "Help me get him out. Why are you standing there gawking?"

Slade shrugged, then lifted one of Luke's arms. "Where you takin' him?"

She pointed to the door. "Out."

Together, she and Slade pulled him through the door. Tugging him to the edge of the porch, she gave a gigantic shove. When he rolled off the porch, dropping four feet into the shrubbery, she ran back into the house and the pool of water in the utility room. Pulling off her flannel jacket, she let it soak up as much water as it could, then ran to the porch and wrung it out directly over Luke's head. She repeated the process until the floor was dry then checked to see how things were going outside.

Buck and Slade were trying to awaken Luke, who lay on his back in the shrubs, his face and hair wet and muddy from Candy's water.

Suddenly, Candy couldn't stand the sight of any of them. "I want you to take your buddy and get out of here," she yelled. "All of you. I don't trust anyone anymore, and what's more, I don't have anything for you to do."

Candy saw Chance's white van arrive at his house. Apparently hearing the ruckus, he came over and stood silently, listening to Candy's tirade.

Slade stood with his straw hat in hand. "You'll call us when you're ready for us again?" he asked in a quiet voice.

"No, I won't call you. I won't be in business. So just take that thing," she gave a disgusted glance at the again-sleeping Luke, "and get out. Go find someone else to work for and be sure to get that bum on the payroll, too."

Finally, she saw Chance and waggled a finger at him. "And you!" she bellowed. "Get off my property and don't come back. Ever!"

She turned to run back into the house, then stopped. "What took you so long?" she yelled over her shoulder. "Where did you stash the stuff, anyway?"

Chance's eyes showed shock, but Candy wasn't about to be fooled. She ran into her house and fell onto the bare stairs, crying. She had tried so hard. Why this? A big sunshiny figure popped into her mind jumping into the white van. She could have stood anything if he had just proved true. And she had finally gotten the faith to believe he was innocent. Great body-wracking sobs shook her small form. How could she hurt this much and continue breathing?

Deciding to go home, she stood up but her knees felt weak. She forced herself to walk toward the door. One step at a time, she told herself. Before she reached the door, it opened and Chance came in. They stood face to face, watching each other silently, like two animals sizing each other up.

eighteen

What did he want with her now? He must know she had seen him climb into his van and leave like an Indy driver. Maybe he thought she was a total fool. But after seeing him take off like that, then finding her carpets gone, even a fool could figure out what happened.

"Why are you here now," she whimpered, "to gloat over me?"

"No." It was almost a whisper. "I want you to tell me what happened." He tried to take her in his arms but she shook him off, stepped away, and turned to face him.

"You don't have to do that anymore. I surrender. It's all yours."

He stepped back. "Please, tell me what you're talking about."

She pointed at the door. "Get out. And don't come back."

He didn't move.

She gave his chest a violent shove. "I mean it, Chance."

He stood firm against her attack. "I called the police—and the hospital—about Sancho."

Sancho—she had all but forgotten him. "How is he?" Her mind whirled again. "We don't need him to tell us who did it now, do we?"

Chance grasped her shoulders and shook her gently. "You must tell me what happened, Candy."

She stood to her entire five feet and looked into his eyes. "Chance, I saw you leave with my carpets this morning. You saw me, too. Why play games anymore?"

He groaned. "Tell me exactly what you saw this morning and

when?"

"I'm not telling you anything. Nor the police. They can't even find the white van that ran Sancho down. The white van, Chance. Does that ring a bell?"

"Of course, it rings a bell." His voice began to rise but how could his eyes remain so clear and innocent? "What kind of idiot do you think I am?" he added.

"You tell the police whatever you want. I fired my whole crew and I'm going home." She pushed past him and ran to her car.

At home she tried to take a nap, watch game shows, and read. She couldn't even think about her enormous debt, but only of Chance's deception. She threw down the book and stormed to the kitchen to make a batch of bread. She could have stood anything, even losing her whole business, if Chance had just been true. She dumped hot water, sugar, salt, and yeast into the bowl, then the flour. Kneading the dough and pounding on it with all her strength, her hostilities abated.

She felt numb, exactly as she had felt after her parents' deaths. Why wouldn't she? Her love had just died—for a man who had used her unmercifully.

Finally, she called the hospital. Sancho still lived but hadn't regained consciousness.

As the afternoon wore on, Candy formed a plan. Chance knew she had fired her crew so he would return to her unguarded house tonight. Probably chop down her curved stairway. She would sneak in, catch him, and make him tell her why.

The afternoon finally crept past and Judy came home. "You should have heard the gloom today, Can, and eating without you was unreal."

"I'll bet Chance was the gloomiest of all."

"He was, Can. He acted as if he'd just lost his last friend."

"You got the right word, Judy. He acted."

Judy spread butter on a thick slice of hot bread and took a bite. "Fantastic, Can." She held up the bread. "It's been a long time."

Candy smiled for the first time since Judy came home. "I took out my anger on the bread."

"Tell me what happened."

"Chance, Judy! I saw him stealing my carpets. With my own eyes."

Judy shook her head as she reached for another slice of warm bread. "No, you didn't, Can. I thought we had that all settled."

Candy felt her body stiffen. "I went to the house really early," she said. "As I pulled into the driveway I saw Chance jump into his van. He tore out of there like he'd seen a ghost—me."

Judy took a long drink of milk and set the glass down. "It wasn't Chance."

"Do I know him or what?" Candy asked. "How often have I seen him this summer? Thirty, forty—one hundred times? His broad shoulders and tiny hips, Judy? How many men are as tall? How many men drive a beat-up white van? How many men wear that blue-and-red flowered shirt? Do you know the shirt?"

Judy scrunched down in her chair. "I know the shirt. He wears it in the mornings, over another shirt. Then he takes it off when he gets too warm. But it wasn't Chance, Can. I thought you finally got that into your head."

A strange frightened look crossed Judy's face. "Know something, Can? Larry's been saying some things that bother me a lot—about you needing to be brought down to size, that you need to go bankrupt. And a lot more. Today I told him I was going to tell you and he sounded so mean he scared me."

Candy jumped up. "See, Judy, it is Chance and Larry knows

it."

Judy's face grew bright red. "You claim to be such a great Christian and go to church every single week, but how many times has God told you it isn't Chance? You're not only hurting Chance, Can, you're wrecking your relationship with God." A white pallor slowly pushed the red from her face. "It's not Chance, but I'm not sure it isn't Larry," she whispered. "I'm never going to be alone with him again." Her shoulders sagged and she plodded off to her room.

After setting her alarm for three-thirty in the morning, Candy hurried to bed. She couldn't sleep after the earful Judy had just given her. Sometimes that kid knew more than she. She really thought God had told her—lots of times—that it wasn't Chance. But seeing is believing!

Before long, a small tap on the door interrupted Candy's dark thoughts. Judy came in and stood by the bed. "Look, Can," she said, "this is how it is with faith. When trouble comes we discover we don't have as much faith as we thought." And then she continued:

"The sun shines on. Skies are blue.
Not a problem mars the view.
Life is full, God is good.
Birds trill away in field, in wood.

Winds arise. Clouds scud on breeze.
Days grow dark. Fear comes—faith flees.
He's gone! Where'd He go?
Left all alone. I loved Him so.

'Wait my child. I'm still here.
Break the darkness, rout the fear.'

Darkness stays, storm rages on.
Lean on Him. Faith grows strong.

Winds abate, sun shines bright.
He's with me day and night.
I love Him so my heart feels sore.
Praise His name. He loves me more."

"Did you just write that?" Candy asked.

Judy shook her head. "God wrote it for me. Lean on Him, Can, and you'll make it through this. And remember, Chance isn't the one." She leaned over and kissed Candy on the cheek. "Now, go to sleep. Things will look better in the morning." She put the poem in Candy's hand and tiptoed out.

Candy reread the poem and almost decided not to go out into the night. But she had to know why Chance had done all this to her. She had to know.

Candy finally slept but when the alarm buzzed, she jumped up, wide awake and full of energy, marveling at how calm she felt. Physically unafraid of Chance, she just wanted to actually catch him stealing or vandalizing. Then, she'd confront him. Her mind turned off at that point.

She pulled quietly into the driveway of the house and coasted to a stop. The van was already there! Backed right up to the door. She wondered what he was taking now.

Dawn hadn't touched the eastern sky yet, and the moon had long ago gone to bed. Stars glittered brightly, trying in vain to light up Candy's world. Her mood matched the black night. She had some choice things ready to say when she had Chance cornered.

Creeping in, she took off her shoes so they wouldn't click,

then tiptoed up the bare stairs, trying to see in the darkness. Then, she waited.

It didn't take long. She heard him in the kitchen, then saw his shadowy form doing something to the cabinets. Crouching on the top step, she held her breath. Not more than fifteen feet from her, he seemed to be turning screws. A moment later, he pulled the oven from the wall and started toward the stairs carrying the huge appliance.

Where could she go? He would hear her if she breathed, let alone moved.

He stopped, and the breeze fanned her as he set the heavy appliance down. He raised up, sighed, and pulled something from his pocket. A moment later, a match flared, lighting his face—it wasn't Chance!

"Slade! What are you doing?" she asked, jumping to her feet.

Slade dropped the cigarette on the vinyl floor and flipped around, looking for her in the dark.

"I'm here, Slade. Why did you take the oven out?"

He attacked the sound of her voice, grabbed her, and locked her head in a tight grip under his arm.

"Slade, stop it. You're hurting me!" Bent and twisted sideways, with all her weight on her neck, she had no leverage.

"Slade, let me go!" She tried to kick him, but couldn't reach. "What are you doing, anyway?" she asked when she gathered in enough air.

He held her until she stopped thrashing. "Why'd you have to come down here for?" he rasped out. "Smashin' a dumb Mexican ain't nothin', but I didn't want to hurt you."

Candy's mind popped. Slade was the man, not Chance! Pain shot through her back and her neck felt as though it would break any minute. She'd never been so happy in her entire life! She felt as though the sun were shining brightly and birds singing in every tree. Nothing mattered if Chance really loved her. She couldn't care less what happened now that she knew Chance wasn't involved.

"Slade, why did you do this?" she asked quietly, her head hanging in front of the big man, the rest of her dangling behind him.

He tightened his hold on her neck, causing more pressure on the back of her head. "I got sick of you, you know-it-all woman," he growled. "You never listened to me once. Thought you was so smart with your newfangled ideas. I been building thirty years and you never listened to me once. I hired on to help you make that business go but you didn't want no help. I didn't want to hurt you, but now I hafta and you deserve it all."

"But I saw Chance tear out of here yesterday morning."

"Quite a trick," Slade sneered. "Would have worked, too, if you'd stayed home tonight. I wasn't comin' back no more after tonight."

Candy felt herself weakening but struggled fiercely, determined not to lose consciousness. She began to care what happened after all. Would Slade kill her? He tightened his hold more and bright lights danced around her face.

His voice seemed to be coming from a distance. "I borrowed Chancellor's shirt from the picnic table one afternoon and wore it for my night work. The van? I had that thing years before Chancellor got his."

Candy couldn't answer but gave a mighty twist and landed a solid kick on his shin with her bare heel.

Slade jumped. "Ouch! Never stop, do you? Well, I'm haulin' you to a spot I have in mind. I'll gag you so tight you won't get three breaths. Then I'll leave you to think about shovin' yourself into a man's world where you ain't needed or wanted. Get movin'." He dropped her to her feet and Candy felt something sharp poking into her back. She tried her best to walk. They negotiated the stairs slowly, and turned toward the front door.

"If you don't want this knife in your back clean up to its pearl handle, you'd best not yell or try to escape when we get outside. Ain't no one around to hear you, anyways."

As he reached for the door, it burst open and a flashlight blinded them.

"All right, Kirkwood," Chance's rich voice yelled. "I have a gun. Let Miss Hartwell go, or I'll blast your rotten brains all over the wall."

Slade hesitated a moment then gave Candy a mighty shove— into Chance—and bolted the other way. Two seconds later the utility room door slammed, followed by silence.

Chance grabbed Candy and looked her over with the flashlight. "Are you all right? Did he hurt you?"

"Stop Slade!" she yelled. "He'll be coming around front for the van."

Chance ran to the front porch just as the van came to life and tore away.

When he turned to Candy, she melted into his arms. "I'm sorry, Chance," she whispered. "How could I have doubted you? And God!" Then she remembered Slade. "Call the police. He'll leave the country if we don't get him quick."

Five minutes later, they waited in Chance's Bronco at Haddell Corner. "I wish they'd hurry," he said, impatiently. "Let's go get him. I can handle Kirkwood."

Candy cuddled against him. "We're waiting. After all we've been through, I'm not losing you now." She pulled his face down to hers for another sweet kiss. "I can't take it in yet," she said. "We're free to love."

A siren interrupted and they craned their necks backwards. Five police cars raced past slowing only slightly to make the